# Katie

#  Chapter One

I don't even get the time to drag my suitcase up the stairs as my step-dad is ushering my mom into the car. I spent my first year at Canaday Hall at Harvard, and now the only thing I get is a wink from my step-dad and a small peck on my cheek from my mom before she whispers, "Be nice to your brothers." Step-brothers.

I was happy for my mom when she remarried, but I didn't realize I was getting two older brothers as well. Even though there was an age difference of over ten years, they never minded babysitting when I was younger. I remember how they played with me and how at every possible opportunity, they pulled me onto their laps.

I was closest with Carter, the oldest of the two. He just turned thirty-two last winter. Carter moved out when I was thirteen, and I haven't seen him since. This changed the dynamic in the house and Brad and I drifted apart.

So now, with my parents away for the summer. It's just me and my step-brother Brad.

As I wave off my mom and dad, a chill rakes through my body, and I quickly try to shake it off as I lock the door behind me.

Wait, whose bag is that?

They are both here. Shit.

My heart pounds in my chest, and a blush rises on my cheeks. When I was younger, I had the biggest crush on Carter. He was my hero, and I was broken when he left. Well, as broken as a thirteen-year-old could be.

I made up this fantasy in my mind, about us marrying one day and live happily ever after. But now, I know that it can never be. I'll still have my dreams, one that have kept me company on many nights.

Dreams that I'll never tell anyone. Thoughts you shouldn't have about your own brother. But I can't control my dirty mind.

This was the reason why I broke all contact with him when I went to Harvard. I needed to focus on my studies and pushed everyone away. Never daring to let any boy near because this little voice in the back of my mind kept whispering I should wait. So, I did. I waited and still do.

It can be somewhat lonely, but I still managed to make some great friends. All who were swooning over the Christmas pictures from Brad and Carter. I wish I never opened that email, because the dreams that followed...

Carter's laughter stops my trail of thoughts and makes my eyes peel away from his bag, I muster up the courage to follow the sound of his voice. Butterflies tickle my stomach and this sense of excitement follows.

Carter and Brad chat away on the couch in the living room. A smile lifts on my lips as I move closer.

Even though I haven't seen Carter since he moved out, Brad had spent plenty of time with him in London. I thought he would stay there eventually, but he always came back home. I don't know why, and maybe I never will.

"There she is," Carter says, holding out his hand for me to take, and I hesitantly take it.

A squeal leaves me when he pulls me closer until I'm planted on his lap. My body freezes, but when I see the way he smiles, it makes something stir inside me. As if I am a kid again, doing everything possible to make him smile.

Letting out a breath, I relax slightly. His arm snakes around my waist, tugging me closer until I feel the outline of his dick pressed against my ass. I squirm forward to escape this sense of unease, but his grip tightens.

"I like it when they fight," Carter whispers.

A blush creeps on my cheeks as embarrassment takes over. I have been in this position plenty times before, and I never saw anything wrong with it. Except I know better now.

His warm breath teases my neck, his cock pressed against me, and his finger gently brushing over my hip, I know I have to get out of here. This isn't what I want. I might have wondered about it, but this is wrong. Too wrong.

"Relax. I'll keep you safe," Carter says.

But what does he mean by safe? Safe in his arms? Under his touch?

"Are you staying here for the entire summer?" I ask, already knowing the answer but hoping this will build some space between us and make me forget about his teasing touch.

Brad watches us, his eyes raking over my body, lingering on the hem of my skirt before taking another sip of his drink.

The heat in his eyes, the way he wets his lips, makes my breath quiver. I have seen that look before, but never with him.

"Yes, Katie. The entire summer," Carter says. "How's school?"

Tucking my hair behind my ear, I lean slightly forward to create space as his breath keeps fanning my ear.

"It was great. But it's good to be home." My skin heats as his caresses continue.

"When are you going to work for me, doll?"

The nickname makes me gulp, and I slowly peel myself away. "It's going to take a while before I can work at your firm." I laugh. It would be a dream come true to work with him in London.

Not with him, or maybe it is, but the idea of working at one of the top law firms in the world is every lawyer's dream.

He hums and takes the glass of whiskey Brad offers. His hold slackens, and I breathe in relief.

"Guys, I'm exhausted." I pause as I get from his lap. "Great to have you back, Carter. See you guys tomorrow." I don't dare to glance back as I feel their stares burning in my back.

"Didn't you miss him?"

Brad's voice forces me to a stop, and I turn to meet his gaze.

"Of course, how can I not?" I joke as Carter walks out of sight.

Brad moves in front of me, blocking my way as his eyes drift over my body. The corner of his lip slightly curves and the smell of whisky invades my senses.

The top buttons of his shirt are open, showing his strong chest. His hair isn't as neat as I'm used to. As if he raked his fingers through it too many times.

"You've been drinking," I say.

"I had to try. See if it would help with my control."

My brows pinch together as his words confuse me. He edges closer until his body is inches away from mine. He lifts his hand but pauses next to my cheek. His fingers flex slightly, and he sighs before moving back.

I take my moment, and rush past him. My steps are sloppy as I hurry up the stairs. I trip over my feet as I hear Brad calling after me, but the voice in the back of my mind screams at me, ordering me to hide in my room before something else happens.

Running inside my bedroom, I lock the door and edge back. My eyes focus on the hall light that shines under the door.

The wiggle of the doorknob makes me hold my breath. I don't dare to make a sound. My heart stammers, the beat ringing in my ears. Heavy footsteps slowly leave the other side of my door, and the shadow goes with it.

Dreams and fantasies are meant to stay hidden and not taken to the real world.

The beating of my raging heart slows. Leaning back, expecting to feel the wall behind me, I bump against someone. The scream that wants to escape gets stuck in the back of my throat as a strong hand covers my mouth. His other arm snakes around my waist, hauling me up until I feel his entire body.

"Struggle for me, doll," Carter whispers.

# CHAPTER TWO

Tears brim my eyes as I try to break free, screaming against his calloused hand, begging the universe for someone to save me.

He groans behind me, his hand leaving my mouth and trailing back to grab my hair and shove me onto my bed.

"Scream. Beg." He snickers. "No one will save you. Not until I'm done with you."

Yanking my skirt over my ass, he inhales sharply. Dipping his fingers between my ass, curling down until he pushes against my entrance. I whimper, thrashing beneath him as he presses my face into the mattress.

"No one has touched you before?" he asks, removing his fingers from my slit.

"Please, let me go. I won't tell anyone. I swear." I continue to fight and his grip on me tightens.

He says nothing but the sound of him fumbling with his pants leaves me shaking.

"It's going to be okay. I promise."

"Please don't. I'm still a virgin. Please, I'll do anything else—" I realize my words fall on deaf ears when I feel his hard cock against me.

My body trembles in panic as he tries to soothe me. "I'll be gentle, only this time."

He lines his dick against my entrance and slowly pushes in. His grip on my hair falterers as he parts my legs further.

I keep them pressed together, trying to win this battle.

"You're too tight. Part your legs for me, doll."

Sobs escape me, and I shake my head, trying to crawl away from the monster behind me.

He grabs my hips and yanks me back. His cock thrusts inside me, and I scream in pain. He tilts his body forward, and his strong chest presses against my back, caging me in as he begins his movement.

"Shhh, now, I know you can take my thick cock. You wouldn't want to disappoint your brother."

Whimpers follow as I can't stop my chest from aching to his words, hating how there is this voice inside my head urging me to please Carter—as I always wanted to when I was younger. Trying to do my best just for him.

"No, no, stop," I beg as his pace increases.

"I'll never stop, doll. I'll make you feel good; you'll see." More empty words fall from his lips, attempting to calm me.

His thrust changes into something filled with an animalistic need. He tilts my hips, giving him more room to go harder, and I cry. The pain I thought was lost comes crashing back.

I move and fight with all my might, but all he does is laugh and moan. His cock hardens as a result of my pleas.

"I knew you would feel this good. We got all the time in the world to turn you into our personal little slut, just as I always imagined it."

His words frighten me to my core, leaving me without words as he continues his attack. My body goes numb beneath him, relaxing as he does what he wants. Until his hand snakes around my hip, trailing to my mound, and I stiffen slightly.

"You'll learn to love this. I'll make sure of it."

"Please, Carter, stop." Tears stream down my cheeks, but it entices him further.

"I should have never left. So much to learn and so little time." Regret laces his words, and his fingers press on my clit. "I'll make it better."

A familiar feeling rises inside me, and I whimper as I know he's forcing me to climax. Forcing my body to like what he's doing to me.

Pulling my lips behind my teeth to stop the sounds of my pleasure from escaping, I clench my eyes shut.

He knows what I'm doing as a dark chuckle leaves him, his lips inches from my ear.

"Don't hold back next time." He groans, and his cock twitches inside me, filling me with spurts of his cum.

Disgust rakes through me. His grip falters, and I crawl away from his touch. I don't want to look at him, but my eyes move on their own. Taking in his lust-filled expression, his eyes wandering over my exposed and bruised skin. He bites his lower lip and inches closer, but the harsh knock on my door stops him.

"Saved by little bro." Carter laughs and scampers up. "If you scream, I'll stuff your mouth with his cock next."

I silently nod, swallowing the lump in the back of my throat, and watch him leave me. Darkness surrounds me, and I wince as I get out of bed.

Exhaustion is ready to take over, but I need my phone first. I need to get out of here. I tip-toe around my room in search of the last remainder of hope.

If I can just find it and call someone, call for help. Everything will be fine.

It turns into a mantra, a silent whisper as anxiety reaches higher.

My steps are without a sound and sobs threaten to escape when I realize he has taken my phone.

The light in the hall goes on, and I hurry into bed, pulling the covers to my chin as I peek through my lashes to see if he'll return. Or maybe it's my other brother.

The door creaks as it opens. Heavy footsteps move closer, and the light casts a hue around the dark silhouette. A silhouette I'll recognize for the rest of my life.

I flinch as Carter brushes his knuckles over my tear-stained cheek. "You look so beautiful broken, Katie."

He pauses as his gaze flickers to my lips, and I inch back. The small act makes him smile, and his touch leaves me. "Come, let's get you cleaned up."

I watch him move into the bathroom. The sound of water running and Carter's hums make me slowly step out of bed, my eyes shifting between the bathroom door and my bedroom door.

Maybe I can run. Maybe I can hide.

I try and run.

My fingers trail over the doorknob as my feet leave the floor. Carter lifts me up and I scream at the top of my lungs. Kicking and fighting with all the strength I have left and all he does is laugh as he takes me to the bathroom.

The hot water engulfs me as he lowers me in the tub. My cries silence as I know I have lost.

Again.

# CHAPTER THREE

He never leaves, guarding me as I sleep and watching my eyes flutter open as the first ray of sun shines through the drapes.

"How are you feeling?" he asks, leaning forward.

Concern is edged on his features, and I wonder if he has any regrets. Maybe he didn't mean it. Perhaps it will never happen again, and this will all be a nightmare. One I can bury deep inside my mind.

The once sophisticated big brother, with his black hair and piercing blue eyes now looks like a different person. The care I always saw in his gaze, have changed into something else.

Something forbidden.

Or maybe, I am the one that misjudged his glances in the past.

My lips won't move as I pull the covers tighter around me.

"Answer me, doll."

His nickname for me makes me realize he knows exactly what he has done. There is no regret. Not when he dares to call me that again.

"Scared," I whisper honestly.

He hums and rises to his feet. The bulge in his pants makes me inch back.

No, not again.

"Are you sore?" He sits beside me, tugging the covers from my naked body. My body trembles as he palms my ass.

"Yes, it hurts."

The lust in his eyes makes me whimper. "I'm really trying to be gentle, but you make it impossible. Shaking and whimpering, I can make you feel better."

"No, please, Carter. You don't have to do this." I make the mistake of pulling back my leg, exposing a part I wanted to keep hidden.

His lips curve, and he sighs. "Then why are you wet?"

I shake my head, trying to shield myself from his burning gaze.

He pulls my leg further apart, exposing my broken pussy.

"Fuck." He breathes. "Look at you."

Trying to close my legs, I lose. With both hands, he pushes them further apart, forcing me on my back. I struggle, trying to crawl away, but he is too strong.

"Do you remember what I used to do when you hurt yourself?

My breath lodges in the back of my throat, knowing what he means.

"Kiss it better." My voice is nothing more than a weak whisper as his eyes are focused on my throbbing pussy.

"Kiss it better," he repeats.

I shake my head and claw at his hands, watching as he inches closer and then presses his wet tongue on my pained slit.

"No," I whimper. His tongue carefully caresses every pained part of me, softening the ache until he flicks it over my clit, and my hips move on their own, bucking against his touch.

He does this again and again until my core spasms in need, my own body deciding it wants this while my mind wants to escape.

I cover my mouth with my hands, not wanting him to hear a sound that comes from my lips as he focuses on my clit.

Carter swirls his tongue around, closing in until his full attack on my clit begins. There is a gentleness to it, and my orgasm starts to form. I try to fight it, push it back with all my might, but he must sense it as he changes his movements. Altering it with slight sucks and teasing my entrance with his fingers, brushing over my slit.

My left leg is free, but as much as I try to fight what he is doing, my back arches from the mattress, and I moan against my hand.

He chuckles, the sound vibrating around my bundle of nerves, and then comes my undoing.

"Good fucking girl."

He sucks again, flicking his tongue, and my orgasm explodes. I cry, my thighs quivering as wave after wave of ecstasy flows through me. Bringing this sense of peace until my juices spill out, covering his face.

"Fuck, doll, I can't wait for you to ride my face and spill over me again."

I swallow hard as his words engrave in my mind. My juices glisten on his face as he crawls over me, reaching my nipples with his skilled tongue, and my cheeks redden in shame.

He forced me to climax, and I can't deny this heat that builds in my core as my walls spasm around nothing.

"You did so good, doll," he whispers against my skin, nibbling on my perked nipple as the sensation snaps to my clit, and I struggle not to lean into his touch.

This is wrong, so wrong.

"I'm so proud of you."

My heart swells, the words I heard many times before when I was younger.

"I know I shouldn't. I need to give you some time." He pauses and fumbles with his pants. "But I need to be inside you again."

"Carter, don't." My bottom lip quivers, and tears brim my eyes as he ignores me again. His thick cock pushes against my wet entrance. The soreness is still there, and I whimper when he slides inside me.

"Shhh, doll. I got you." He buries his face in the crook of my neck, his hands on my hips as he moves out so slowly. My walls stretch and wrap around him and clench when he tilts his hips.

A satisfying groan escapes him, and goosebumps rise on my heated skin. I lay, not knowing what else I can do as I feel my body responding to his touches.

"We can climax together," he whispers.

I shake my head. "I want you to stop." My voice doesn't sound like my own; my back curves as another orgasm coils in my core. Building as his pelvis pushes against my clit with every deep thrust he makes.

"I will if you come with me."

My jaw clenches, and I close my eyes, pushing back all that rises beneath my skin. He releases my hip, his fingers teasingly trailing to my clit.

"But you will come, doll. I promise."

I know he is right. I know I can't hold this back anymore. He plays with my clit, his fingers skillfully moving side to side, applying just enough pressure to make my walls spasm.

My orgasm climbs, building, ready to explode. His cock hardens, and the combination of his thrusts and plays makes a shaky moan leave my parted lips.

My back curves up, my hard nipples rub against his bare chest, and I balance on the thin line of an earth-shattering orgasm. A stray tear rolls down my cheek, and without my intent, I wrap my arms around him, pulling him closer as my legs move around his hips, my heels digging into his ass, and I cry out as my orgasm washes through me.

His follows, stilling deep inside me. His cock twitches as stream after stream of his cum fills me, and I slump back on the mattress.

"You did perfectly. My beautiful little slut."

# CHAPTER FOUR

I can't believe I did that; I stopped fighting. Wiping away the tears, I focus back on the hot water that cascades down my body. Erasing everything that has happened. Washing away my juices and his cum.

Scrubbing my skin until it turns a harsh red, it still doesn't feel like enough. My body and mind are torn. I know this is wrong. He is taking advantage of me; he raped me. But my body craves more. Wanting to be good for him.

How he made that happen, I'll never know. But as my sore pussy tingles in need, I hate it. Or maybe I don't.

I can't deny that I never thought about it, but I never wanted it to be like this.

My spiraling thoughts won't stop; I keep coming back to the same conclusion. This is wrong, but.... But I like the way I feel when I make him proud and the way he makes me come. I never felt anything like that. It isn't like I never touched myself. I did, but I could never let myself build up like that, explode like that.

How does he do that?

I shake the worry-filled thoughts and turn off the shower. As I dry myself, I remember I didn't bring any clothes in the bathroom.

It feels like a week has passed, but it has been one night.

With a towel wrapped around me, I move silently to my bedroom, ready to get dressed and run or something.

"What the fuck?" I whisper as all I see are dresses.

Panic fills me. My insides turn as I search for anything to put on. My suitcase is still downstairs, but I must have something in here to wear. Something that covers me up more.

"You don't need much, doll. I want to have access to you at all times."

"No, you can't do this." I shake my head as anger boils inside me. He took me by force, and now he takes away the last remainder of my dignity.

His lips curve, and he stalks closer. "I can do anything I want."

"No, I don't want this." I move back, but he grabs the towel that covers me, yanking it from my skin.

"Kneel, doll."

My cheeks flush, and I repeat my words, but the way his eyes glint, the hunger that shows, reminds me he likes this. He craves this, the fight. He wants me to say no; he gets off on this. Taking me against my will. The massive bulge in his pants is enough proof.

"Kneel." The nickname is gone, and his jaw ticks. The lust in his gaze changes slightly. The anger rises, and I gulp. Fear prickling as I stand my ground.

He laughs, closing the distance between us and grabbing the back of my head.

"Kneel," he says through gritted teeth as he pushes me to my knees.

I claw at his hand, but he is too strong for me.

He unbuttons his pants and frees his cock. Precum leaks from the tip.

I press my lips firmly against each other.

"Doll, make me proud and open your mouth."

My heart aches at his words, and my eyes snap up at his. My lips peel away from each other, and I slowly open my mouth.

"Such a good little slut."

My core throbs at the sound of his words, my body once again betraying me as wetness pools between my legs.

He rubs the tip of his cock against my lips and moistens them with his pre cum before he slides inside my mouth. The salty taste tickles my tongue, and he pushes deeper until I struggle to catch my next breath.

"Take it," he says and pushes further.

My throat constricts, and I panic. I might throw up. But when I hit that tipping point, he pulls back.

"Breathe through your nose and wrap your lips around it."

His grip on my hair tightens, and I do as he says.

He starts slow, letting me adjust to his size, feeling the tip of his cock curve down my throat, and I swallow.

He groans in pleasure, my nose pressed against his pelvis. My fingers dig into his hips, trying to steady myself as my legs shake.

He moans. "Fuck, you feel great."

Pulling back, his moves change. The softness disappears, and the animal inside him rises. A part I have experienced before.

Lust and rage fill his eyes as he slams his hips back and forth. Forcing me to take everything as he holds the back of my head. I gag and choke. Tears well through my eyes, my lips breaking. My throat aches more with every pound, and I slam my hands on his hips. Pleading him to stop.

I gave in, and it still feels like he is punishing me. What else can I do to make the bad side of this stop? Or did I make it up in my head that there was a good side to this?

My vision dots, my body weakens, and he stills inside me. Pushing his cock as far as possible while his cum spurts down my throat.

With a gentle touch, his thumb brushes over my jaw. "So proud of you."

My heart swells at the sound of those simple words again, and I blink away the blur.

His cock softens, and he pulls out, kneeling before me.

"I own you now. This mouth." He trails his thumb over my broken bottom lip and pulls slightly until I whimper.

"This cunt." His other hand moves down and cups my mound, pressing his digits on my sore and used pussy.

"Fuck, look how wet you are. I knew you would like this." He pushes his digit inside me, and I moan. The soreness still is there, but there is something more.

Something I don't want.

Desire.

"And God, I can't wait to destroy that ass," he says as a grin tilts his lips.

The pain between my legs subsides as something else rises.

His finger reaches deeper. My hips jerk forward, and my walls tighten around his finger, but it isn't enough. I shake my head, feeling it grow. Wanting to feel better, good even.

"Say what you want," he whispers. "It's okay; you can tell me." The palm of his hand presses on my clit as his digit work inside me.

I shake my head, angry at myself for riding on his hand. I need, I need...

More.

"Please, Carter." This isn't a plea for him to stop; it's for him to continue.

He smiles, his other hand snakes around my waist, and he pulls me closer, his lips hovering over mine. "My perfect little slut."

Something shifts between us. A barrier has been destroyed as he guides me on my back. The fluffy carpet teases my skin, and he parts my legs as far as possible. His gaze locks on my glistering slit. I could never stop the wetness from forming; I could never stop my body from craving its release—a release only he can give me.

He lines his cock, and slams inside me without warning. I cry out in pain, my body shaky as I try to crawl away, not being able to handle this deepness.

He grins, grabbing my hips and pushing my legs over his shoulder, leaning closer as tears form in my eyes. The harshness of his attack leaves me panting, and I claw at his shoulders.

"Stop, you're hurting me."

He shakes his head, slowly retreats his cock, and slams back inside—forcing me to whimper.

"Shhh, doll," he says as he brushes his knuckles over my hip. "You're doing great. Such a good little slut."

His hand drifts lower until I feel him pressing his finger on my ass. "This is next." He pushes, and I'm unable to move away until his finger plops inside me.

My back curves, and my body trembles as my walls spasm around his pumping cock. The sensation of feeling something in both places leaves me breathless, and my orgasm coils inside me, ready to break free.

My ass relaxes, and he adds another digit, stretching me for what he's planning. Tension crawls under my skin; my toes curl as I cannot hold it back any longer.

It starts slow. Electricity crackles inside me, my climax rising as I moan in ecstasy. Forgetting about all the bad he put me through, I focus solely on the pleasure his touch brings.

"Scream, doll," he says as he stretches me further.

I do as he says, unable to hold anything back. A stray tear falls, and I cry out. My insides change; everything changes when I accept this fully.

There is no escape from this, but did I even try to run?

Sweat coats my skin as another orgasm builds, his attack is too much for me to handle as I ride on this moment of pure pleasure. My body craves everything he gives, and I hate and love it at the same time.

And now, as I arch my back further, as he guides his cock into my ass, I whimper and plead.

His dick hardens further, and he laughs. He pushes deeper and deeper until there is nothing more to give. Everything throbs, my breath comes out in pants, and he is silent.

He says nothing, does nothing, and I dare to glance back. His eyes are locked on my ass, the palm of his hand gently rubbing it. And I don't know what to do. Did I do something wrong?

"Carter?" I whisper, and his eyes snap to mine.

"You are doing so much better than I thought you would," he says and starts to move.

I bite my lip to hold back the moan when I hear footsteps echo from the hall.

A harsh smack on my ass comes next, and I scream. I try to move forward, but his other hand keeps me in place.

"You don't want our brother to hear that you like my cock inside you, doll?"

I shake my head, and another harsh slap follows.

"Don't you want to know how good it feels to have us both inside you?"

Panic rises at the sound of his words, my insides clench, and Carter groans behind me.

"Hmm, it seems like you want to, but not today. Don't worry, doll."

I exhale in relief, and Carter pushes my face into the carpet as he continues his attack. Keeping his promise to destroy every part of me.

Whimpers escape me as he plummets inside me. Every thrust is harder than before, and the pain is almost too much.

"Please, Carter. You're hurting me."

He yanks my upper body by my hair until my back is flush against him. His arms rake around me, holding me in place as his hips jerk up. He cups my breast, pinching my nipples; an electric pleasure zaps to my clit, one he catches with his other hand, toying with the sensitive bundle of nerves.

My body is in overdrive, unable to focus on one point of pleasure—all of it becoming too much. My walls spasm around nothing as he continues.

"I got you, doll. Let it go," he whispers.

My body tightens, pleasure reaching higher until there is nothing keeping it inside.

I moan.

My orgasm moves through me. "Fuck." My juices squirt out, dripping down my thighs.

"Such a good, good little slut."

# Chapter Five

He was right when he said he wanted easy access. With my dress pulled up around my waist, he pushes inside me as I hold onto the kitchen counter.

I whimper and moan as he takes what he wants, claiming my body as his, over and over again. He never let me leave the house. He never gave me back my phone.

I have tried to leave, but he locked this place down like a prison.

There is no fight left in me, and I have given my body completely to him. He punishes me when he pleases. He fucks me when he pleases, but I know he wants more.

I can feel it in my core, and how he displays me in front of our brother lets me know exactly what he's planning.

He wants Brad to join us, and the thought makes my insides coil. I don't even know if Brad wants to, or maybe he doesn't have a choice like I did—and still don't. I might have accepted it and enjoyed the pleasure it brings me, but even if I wouldn't want it, Carter would still take it.

He has shown me that he will get what he wants, and the more I fight, the more he takes.

As he grabs a fistful of my brown hair, he forces me to watch the door. I can already hear Brad's footsteps coming closer. He went out to get groceries, and now Carter is waiting for him to see us.

To show his little bro how he fucks me and how I have learned to enjoy it.

The door to the hall slowly opens, and Brad walks in, focused on his phone, until he hears me whimper. Carter purposely fucks me harder, forcing more sounds from my lips.

Brad stills and watches us. He swallows thickly and places his phone down.

"Carter," he says.

A flicker of hope ignites inside me. Did I make the wrong assumption? Maybe Brad can get me out of this mess.

"Brad," Carter says as he forces another moan from my lip. "She feels so good."

Brad inches closer, his eyes drifting over my body and lingering on my mound. I don't know what to say, fearing if I say something wrong or if I misjudge this situation, Carter will punish me.

I have felt the pain he can inflict on me, and he enjoys it more than he should. I don't want to fuel the monster inside him.

Brad's hand hovers over my cheek, and I flinch slightly. "She's not ready," he says and peels his fingers away.

The disappointment in his eyes makes my heart ache. A response I also get when Carter is upset with me. I still don't know how he made sure my body would react in these kinds of ways, but it hurts. Everything inside me screams to make them proud.

"She can take you." Carter moans. His fingers trail to my clit, and I hold my breath, knowing what will come next.

My hand snakes around Carter's neck for balance as my hips buck. My orgasms builds, tightening my core, and Carter's moans vibrate over my heated skin.

"Little brother fears he will break you," Carter whispers.

My brows pinch, wondering how Brad could be worse than Carter. Carter already broke me; there is nothing left to break. Right?

My skin prickles, balancing on the edge of climaxing. "Why?"

"Trust me, doll. He's worse than me." He chuckles, and before I can ask further, he pinches my clit, forcing me to fall off the edge.

"God," I scream, my head falling back as my body spasms in his hold. His orgasm follows next, unable to thrust through my clenched walls as they milk him for everything he's got.

With hooded eyes, I meet Brad's hungry gaze, an expression that makes me gulp. He comes closer; his finger brushes over my skin until it dips to my clit.

I hiss when he presses down, trying to inch back as the sensitivity is too much. He ignores my discomfort and toys further without breaking eye contact. He is searching for something.

"You like to be fucked by Carter?" he asks, the harshness in his voice raking through my spine.

I hold my tongue, not wanting to say yes. I want to say no, but that isn't the complete truth.

"It's complicated," I say. Pleasure whirls inside me, my breathing changes, and I know I'm coming closer to another orgasm.

"It's not. With me"—his finger leaves me—"it will be."

My pussy pulsates with need, and I rub my thighs together, feeling Carter's cum drip down my leg and still wanting more.

What has happened to me?

Carter made good on his promise; he made sure I learned to love this and made me into his slut, just as he always imagined.

Brad doesn't look back as he slumps down on the couch.

"Do you want to come again, little slut?" Carter asks, brushing away my hair from my shoulder.

My jaw clenches, and I hate what I'm about to do. Saying the three-letter word I never thought I would say.

"Yes," I whisper.

He groans behind me and pulls the dress over my head, tossing it on the floor without a care.

"I'm so proud of you. My personal little slut."

My heart swells at his words, and I turn in his hold, my hands resting on his chest as he guides me back until my ass hits the kitchen counter.

He might have forced this all on me, forced his desires, his wishes. But now I can't deny I want it too. I want him to make me his, take me as he wants until I'm a broken mess—just for him.

So maybe I was wrong. Maybe it isn't impossible to have your dreams.

No matter how dirty they are.

# CHAPTER SIX

The cold liquid from my glass caresses my dry throat as my eyes burn into hers. Her lids are half closed, her lips parted slightly, and soft moans pour from them. Carter fucks her from behind, groaning like an animal.

I should have taken her when I had the chance. I never should have waited because now, as she is being fucked by my brother on the kitchen counter, all I want to do is rip him away and punish her for letting him fuck her.

I know the idea was to share, and we will, but first, I need some time with her alone. I need to form her into the goddess she can become. I can see it in her eyes; she craves more of this all. She craves to be fucked senseless over and over again until she begs me to stop.

But I won't.

I'll never stop because she isn't the one pulling the strings.

I am.

My cock throbs, straining my pants, and I'm on the verge of losing control. I can't, though. I want to play a game. A wicked game.

The corner of my lips tugs slightly at the idea. I'll give her everything she wants, her freedom, her life back, only to tear it all away again. Destroy the last bit of hope she has.

The hope I know lingers inside. The hope she has in me.

She doesn't realize that my older brother never lied when he said I would be worse.

The number of times Carter had to save me is too many to count. I was young and stupid and gave in to my primal needs hunt.

I know better now; I learned better.

And still, I always get what I want.

I want her tears, her agonizing screams. I want her pain and pleasure. I want to rip her to pieces and sew her back together in the way I want her to be.

Every limit she has set on herself, I'll destroy.

And when I'm done with her, she'll crawl behind me. Begging me to do it again because no one other than me can make her feel like her true self.

A self she hasn't met yet, but I know it exists.

I know who she truly is; not even Carter sees it.

Carter groans loudly and stills inside her, her perked nipples brushing over the kitchen counter with every breath she takes.

The slap on her ass makes her moan, and Carter ushers her upstairs to get cleaned up. She does without complaint, her legs wobbly from the decent fuck.

Carter watches me; he knows how the wheels in my mind work.

"I think she is ready."

"She can never be ready for what I want." I shift in my seat, my cock uncomfortably rubbing against my zipper.

"Come on, little brother. Let's play."

He likes the idea, but he thinks he knows my games. That he has seen them all. However, he forgets I have changed and grown, and so have my urges.

"Let's play."

# CHAPTER SEVEN

## *Katie*

My skin prickles as the hot water caresses my skin, washing away all the dirty acts I had to endure. Endure...

It's a heavy word for something I no longer say no to.

I don't know how I never noticed Carter's ideas of love; maybe it was because he left when I was thirteen. He never showed this side; he only cared for me in his way. But now, as I have seen what he wants, what he craves.

He knew back then what he wanted from me, but then...why leave?

Did his father make him leave? Was there more to the story? How does Brad fit into all of this?

He withdrew from me when Carter left, and all I can remember was my mother telling me that Brad was a loner and that I should just leave him be.

And I did.

I hid in my room, went to school, and did it all over again. My mom and stepdad never truly cared, I think. And I didn't mind; I had a freedom most never experienced.

However, you can't tell me that my stepdad doesn't know his son's dirtiest dreams.

The temperature of the water lowers, telling me I have been standing here long enough. I quickly wash myself and get out, not knowing what I should do next.

Would Carter be waiting for me? Like he has been every day?

The soreness between my legs never vanishes, but it doesn't hurt anymore. Not in a bad way.

I wonder if I will run when he lets me outside.

With the towel wrapped around my body tightly, I step out of my bathroom into my bedroom.

No Carter.

I sigh in relief, but I can't help but feel sad. Disappointed.

Damn, he really did a number on my mind.

I'm losing it if I'm starting to miss him.

As I skim through my closet, my brows knit together. A pair of jeans neatly folded, with a simple black t-shirt.

He said he wanted easy access at all times.

Then what is this?

I don't dwell too long on it and rush to get dressed, not daring to take too long as I fear he would rip them off my skin any minute.

With a clean body and confused thoughts, I go downstairs. My stomach rumbles for some food.

My cheeks blush as my eyes fall on the kitchen island where Carter fucked me yesterday. Electricity runs under my skin, awakening something twisted inside me as flashes of Brad pour through my mind.

I remember what Carter told me, that he would share me with his brother but that I have to be careful because Brad is worse than him.

How though?

How can anybody be worse than what Carter put me through?

"You look nice."

My body tenses as Brad's voice startles me. Is this it? Is this the moment he decides to have a go, a taste, a fuck.

I turn and muster a smile. "Thank you."

He looks normal, not a wicked glint showing in his eyes, not a lust-filled gaze that wanders over my body, one that lingers too long on what's between my legs.

"I thought you would enjoy pants for once." He smiles at me with a tilted head, and I can't help but laugh.

"Sure do."

The tension I had moments ago fades into nothing as I feel safe. Realizing he isn't going to take me here, he isn't going to cross that line.

At least not yet.

I focus back on my needy stomach and open the fridge. My shoulders slump as there is nothing for me to eat, nothing other than a simple sandwich.

"Do you want to go out?"

Is this a test? A trick? Why is he doing this?

I pause, my lips part and close a few times, trying to find the words. Not daring to mess this up.

"I would like that."

"I know just the place." He grabs his keys and gestures for me to lead the way.

My hesitation is there in every step; my nerves rise as I see this as a moment to run.

I thought I was fine with all this, and a part of me is. I like how Carter makes me feel when he takes what he wants.

But I also know this is wrong and twisted. Too dark to be doing my entire life.

We can never be together; no one would look at us the same.

And what would our parents say?

My raging thoughts won't stop, not when I climb into Brad's truck, not when he drives off without a word.

As if he knows what is going on in my head.

"Where are we going?" I manage to ask, hoping that spilling words from my lips will help with these drowning thoughts.

A smile lights on his face. His entire body is relaxed to the fullest. He leans to the side, and with one hand on the steering wheel, he trumps his fingers on the beat of a song by the Rolling Stones.

"Remember that little place we went to when we were younger?"

When we were younger? Nothing comes to mind, not until I recognize the street he is turning onto. "No, we haven't been there since Carter left for England." I can't stop the smile that forms as I see the tiny pancake house at the end of the street.

We used to come here every week until Carter left.

"You remembered," I whisper as I lean forward, afraid the place will vanish if I blink.

I asked my mom so many times if we could go back there, and I always got the same answer.

We don't have time; if you want some Dutch pancakes, you can try to make them yourself.

Maybe I don't remember it right; maybe my mom never took me there.

"It was you and Carter, right?" I ask as he finds a spot to park.

He says nothing, but that is answer enough.

Sometimes, your memories change over time; you miss things or add something that wasn't there.

"Mom and Dad had their own thing." He shrugs as if it's nothing. But it makes me realize what an ass I have been to Brad.

I listened to my mom and let him be while he, too, was missing his brother and what we were to each other.

"I'm sorry that I ignored you," I say.

It's weird to have this kind of normal conversation with how everything is at home, but now it's almost like it isn't there.

"Well, I ignored you too." He chuckles and gets out. He doesn't wait for me as he walks straight to the restaurant.

There it is again, the hesitation.

I can get out and make a run for it, disappear, and never come back. I will be free from whatever they have planned for me.

The idea stops when I see the tension in his legs; he is testing me.

Maybe that's his game. He wants me to run for him.

I shake my head as I get out. My mind is fucked up from all that has happened. And before I do anything, I have to have a plan.

Either a plan to stay and have this as my life, whatever this is.

Or a plan for my escape.

# CHAPTER EIGHT

B rad doesn't hold back when he orders, going all out, and soon the table is filled with all kinds of pancakes, more than we could ever finish by ourselves.

We talk as if we never stopped talking over the years, as if nothing weird is going on at home. And for a brief moment, I forget about it all.

"Why did you never have a girlfriend?"

My question caught him off guard. But with a shake of his head, he answers, "Who said I never had any girlfriends?"

"Well, you never took one home." I would have noticed, or was I that blind?

He hums. "True."

There is something he's not telling me, but I can't figure out what exactly.

"So?"

"What? You want to know where I fucked them? Or how I fucked them?" He stares at me, his gaze piercing and burning into my soul as my breathing hitches in my throat and my cheeks redden.

"No, it's not—"

"What, Katie? What is it that you want to know?"

My words stammer, and I don't know the answer to his question. What do I even want? Truly want.

I sigh in defeat and decide to throw it out there. "Why did Carter say you are worse than him?"

"Eager to find out?"

This is going all wrong, the wrong direction, the wrong intentions. Shit. I didn't mean to get here with my questions because I don't know.

"No, I'm good," I mumble and stuff my mouth with a big bite of my pancake, ensuring I don't dig myself deeper into this hole.

He watches me, and for the first time, his expression changes; his eyes fill with that familiar glint, lust.

His eyes rake over my body, lingering on my breast. "I'm not worse than Carter."

His words surprises me, not at all what I was expecting.

"It's just different but can be very enjoyable for both parties."

Oh, there it is.

"And how different?"

The corner of his lip twitches as he glances at his plate. "I like it when they beg."

I snort and shake my head. I don't see that happening very soon. I might have asked Carter a few times if he could do his thing, but to truly beg? Not happening.

"Good luck with that." I chuckle.

"I like a challenge."

It's funny how normal this seems. It almost makes me forget about how our situation is, what Carter forced upon me.

Maybe this can be my life, but I don't want to stay a captive. Locked in the house the entire day. I have a life and school to get back to.

Brad shuffles a wrapped box over the table and gestures for me to open it when all I did was stare at it with knitted brows.

With a slight hesitation, I open it and freeze. I see it's a brand-new iPhone.

The screen lights up as I touch it, and a picture of Brad and Carter from Christmas in London pops up.

"I set everything up. It's all yours."

I don't know what to say, but I do know my thoughts change.

They go back to running, escaping this all.

Even when I can't peel my eyes away from Carter and Brad smiling, even when something stirs inside me. A warmth that spread beneath my skin.

I know this is wrong.

Too wrong.

My mind is whirling, going back and forth.

"Thank you," I muster.

"It shouldn't have happened the way it did. Maybe we can go back."

"Back? You think Carter doesn't want to fuck me anymore."

"No, he will continue to do that, but I will wait."

"Then you can wait very long."

I feel stronger with Brad, more daring to say what is on my mind. Perhaps it is because I don't have this need to make him proud of me or make him happy with my actions. I never had that with him, only with Carter.

"I won't wait until you say yes; I take what I want. The only thing I wait for is you begging for it."

So, I wonder, what does that mean for his desires?

"I'll be right back," Brad says as he rises.

I silently nod and follow him with my gaze. He's going to the bathroom.

My heartbeat increases, seeing this as an opening.

Where would I go?

Everything inside me screams to run, to at least try. I don't believe they would hurt me if I did, right?

They aren't monsters...right?

I stumble to my feet and run; I don't look back. I don't even know where I'm running to and why.

Why am I running?

No, no, no, it's a good thing I am. I shouldn't be here.

My breathing is sharp; my legs tremble as I pick up my pace. I dial my mother's number, even though I don't even know what to say. Would she even believe me? Would she care?

She must have known what kind of desires my brothers had. I might have been blind, but she couldn't be.

"Hi, angel."

My legs stop, and everything silences around me as my step-father's voice echoes through the phone.

"Angel?"

How could I tell him? They are his sons.

"Hi, Dad," I say as my eyes drifts around me.

"Are you having fun with your brothers? I know you haven't seen Carter in a while, but they haven't been jerks to you, right?"

My mind is blank, my lips frozen. What do I say?

"Katie? Tell me if they misbehaved." His voice changes, and a harshness runs through it.

"No, everything is fine." I couldn't do it. He wouldn't believe me.

"Great, your mom and I have a reservation. I will let her know you called. Bye, Katie."

"Bye, Dad."

The phone goes silent, and the bit of hope I had crumbles.

The sound of cans falling in the distance makes my breath quicken. The darkness in the alley makes me shiver.

Putting the phone in my back pocket, I turn to go another way, but before I can, a hand is placed over my mouth, and I'm pushed against the cold brick wall to my side.

I fight in his grasp more than I ever did. He turns me and slams me against the wall. My back bruises on impact, my head takes a hit, and my sight blurs for a moment.

The stranger wears all black, a hood shielding his face from mine, but the scent he carries will be one I never forget.

Cedarwood.

It's strong, surrounding his body as a thick blanket.

His hand wraps around my throat, squeezing enough for me to struggle with my next breath.

"Stop, don't do this, let me go!" The brick wall scratches my back as I fight in this man's hold.

I kick my legs, but he won't move an inch. I claw at his hand, but all I hear are groans. Groans that I recognize. He's getting off on this.

The man rips away my pants, destroying it fully until I feel the night breeze brush past my pussy.

I shouldn't have run; I should have stayed with Brad, and this wouldn't have happened.

The man turns me, pressing my face against the wall, and I whimper in pain as he thrust his fingers inside me without warning. He stretches me, adds another finger, and starts pumping.

My body shakes in fear. I try to close my legs, but he makes it impossible. His knees keep mine open as he continues his harsh attack.

His fingers hit that sweet spot inside me, and I try to fight it, focusing on the fear, not daring to let it go.

I don't want to come.

I don't want to come.

I blame Carter. My body doesn't mind being fucked against my will; it will still climax.

My walls clench and pulsate, and he knows. He knows I'm close.

I shamelessly tilt my hip back, ready on the verge of climaxing, hoping it will be over after that. But then, his touch disappears.

Everything fades.

I don't dare to move. I listen and wait until I'm sure I'm alone.

Tears roll down my cheeks; a sob leaves me as I turn. My body is sore, my face has scratches from the wall, and wetness drips down my legs.

There isn't enough of my clothes left to walk somewhere decent. I'm stuck here in this filthy alleyway.

I try to make the best of my clothes, and that is when I see it.

The phone Brad gave me.

More tears fall as I realize what my only option is.

I have to call them to pick me up; that is the only way out of this.

Shame is all I feel as I slide down, curling my arms around my legs.

I don't know who to call, but my first choice is Carter.

The dial tone is all I hear until the click of the voicemail.

I try again, but nothing.

Leaving me with one more choice.

Brad.

# Chapter Nine

Breathing through my trembles, I call him.

After two tones, he picks up, and all I hear is his breathing.

"I need help," I whisper, not sure what to say. Do they even want to know what happened? I don't even know what happened.

"Why?"

My ribs clench around my lungs while I fight the tears; I don't want him to hear it. I don't want him or Carter to see me weak.

"I shouldn't have run, I'm sorry."

"But why should I pick you up?"

"You can do whatever you want to me." Why did I say that? I don't want anyone to touch me, but I need him to come get me.

"Who says I want to fuck you?" His words sting and I try to shake it off.

I know he wants me; I have seen it. I have seen the thick bulge in his pants when he thinks I don't see him looking.

And then I realize.

I know what he wants; he told me that earlier.

"Please, Brad, please come get me."

Soft laughter flows through the phone. "Beg harder."

I swallow the reminder of my pride and do as he asks.

"Brad, please come get me. I need you here. Please." Sobs fall; nothing is keeping me together anymore.

There is a moment of silence, and all I hear are my own cries.

"Where are you?" There is a softness in his voice, one that soothes my trembling body.

"I don't know, in an alleyway."

He hums, and I hear his truck come to life. The same song as before fills his car, creating a sense of safety.

He is coming to get me, and then everything will be okay.

As my body won't stop trembling, I hear footsteps coming closer. I hold my breath, begging that it isn't the stranger from before.

"Katie?" Brad's voice is soft as he crunches down before me.

He tucks my hair behind my ear and forces me to tilt my head as he hooks his fingers under my chin.

With a gentle brush over my cheek, I still whimper.

"Come, let's go home," he whispers, and his arms snake around me. I hold on tight as he lifts me and takes me out of the darkness.

He asks nothing while I'm curled up in his arms. I sigh in relief when I see his truck waiting for us.

As he puts me in the passenger seat, he gives me his jacket, shielding me from the night.

His big jacket clings to my bare body. And I wait for him to ask what happens when he drives away, heading home.

Perhaps I should tell him, but what can I tell?

Some guy finger fucked me until I almost came, and then he left me.

And now, even with my mind in shame, my stupid pussy needs to come. I blame Carter. He made sure my body craved the roughness, the harsh fuck.

I squirm in my seat, ashamed of the feeling between my legs.

"What's wrong?" Brad asks.

"Nothing," I mumble and lean back.

"Don't lie," he warns, his voice harsh and stern, the same tone as I heard before from his father.

"He touched me," I whisper.

"I know." He takes my hand, peeling it away from my body, and brushes his thumb soothingly over my skin.

My body relaxes, and the trembling fades.

"What did he do?" he asks, and my body tenses.

"H-he finger fucked me." I breathe fully, somewhat relieved by saying it out loud.

His thumb stops, and his hold on my hand tightens. "Did you come?"

I clench my jaw, hating that he is asking me this. "No."

I rub my legs together as my walls vibrate around nothing.

He softly laughs and shakes his head. "So, that's why you are squirming in my seat. I wonder how wet my jacket will be when you give it back."

I yank my hand back and look out of the window. My cheeks flame in embarrassment, hating that he knows.

"It's okay, Katie. I know you can't help it. We all know you liked to be fucked against your will."

"So, you are going to fuck me now?"

He shakes his head with a sigh. "Only if you beg me to."

I'm not that stupid.

"But I'm sure Carter is most willing to let you come."

"You won't?"

"I will only let you come if you behave, and you don't."

I huff and keep my lips sealed until we're home. I want to stuff his jacket in his face. I don't know how he does it, but he's getting under my skin. He is making me angry at him; he's taunting me.

And I hate it.

However, it does make the fear I had moments ago disappear. Even though his words aren't normal, I do feel normal again. At least a bit.

Carter waits for us at the door; worry is edged on his face. Brad must have told him. But why didn't he pick up his phone?

"There she is." He smiles with his arms wide open, waiting for me to run up to him.

Warmth spreads inside me, and a feeling of safety follows. I don't stop myself when I leap toward him, falling into his soothing embrace.

He takes me inside; Brad follows close behind me. They talk to each other, but nothing about what happened to me.

Carter takes me upstairs and peels the remainder of my clothes away. He tries to hide it, but I can see the anger storming in his eyes when he sees the bruises painting my skin.

"Come, let's get you rinsed off, and then we take a bath together." His gentle, caring voice isn't something I heard lately, but it is something I desperately need now.

His touch is soothing, and he doesn't cross any boundaries he has crossed before as he washes my sore body.

But the groan that leaves him when his fingers dip between my legs can't be missed. I slightly tense, and his hand disappears.

"I won't, Katie. I do have some restraint."

"You do?" I joke.

"Very little."

Brad steps into the bathroom without warning and runs the bath. His eyes are blank, even when they rake over my body. Not lingering on any part.

As Carter turns off the shower, Brad extends his hand, wanting to help me into the bath, and I try to push him away.

I sneer. "I can get in myself."

"Ours to fuck, ours to take care of," Carter says.

There is only one fucking me, and the other one only confuses me.

I hum and let it go; let them do what they want to. I don't know if it is to make me feel better or themselves.

"And don't worry, doll. You can ride my face later; I heard you need to come."

I glare at Brad, and all I get in return is a smug smile. Ass.

The hot water soothes my aching body as they slowly drop me in. Carter doesn't wait long and discards his clothes to get in with me.

The bath is big enough for the three of us, and I wonder what Brad will do.

He comes closer, kneels behind me, and puts his lips to my ear.

"You haven't deserved to see me naked yet."

I shiver as his breath teases my wet skin, and then he leaves me alone with Carter.

"Brad likes his games," Carter says, pulling my attention back to his.

"You said he would be worse than you."

"And he is. Trust me on that."

# Chapter Ten

Maybe it shouldn't surprise me that Carter hasn't touched me yet, but how could it not? He has been nothing but caring and nice.

Brad even, in his weird way. I ignore his comments that make me blush or angry.

So now, as we all watch some stupid show on the television, I can't ignore the soft brushes of Carter's fingers on my bare thigh. He's torturing me with this. He must know what he's doing.

He destroyed my body and shaped it into what he wanted, ensuring I would always respond to his touch and needs. Needs that have become my own.

It's stupid and sick that I still want to be touched after what happened in the alleyway. Maybe it's because what that man did wasn't worse than what Carter already has done to me.

And now, I'm the girl with the twisted thoughts.

Carter nudges me as Brad gets up to get something from the kitchen.

"Two can play a game," he whispers.

He leans back, lying on the couch. "Ride my face."

I gulp, and my eyes drift to Brad, who doesn't notice what is happening.

"Don't make me ask twice," Carter warns. A pleasurable shiver runs through me at the harsh tone, and I crawl up his body, lifting the dress over my hip.

My only jeans have been destroyed, so now it's back to dresses with easy access. But for once, I'm not complaining.

I hover over his face as his hands grip my hips, trying to pull me down.

"Sit, Katie," he says.

"I will suffocate you, Carter." My legs shake as his grip tightens.

"Then I will die a happy man; now sit!"

I relax my legs and sit down. His tongue dips inside me, and I moan. Fuck, that feels good.

His nose presses against my clit, as his tongue fucks me, and I start to ride his face.

My sounds make Brad look our way. He freezes, his gaze drifting down, but he can't see anything as the couch armrest shields his line of sight.

I grin as pleasure spreads within me. My nipples perk through the flimsy fabric of my dress, and Brad stalks closer.

My orgasm rises higher, my walls pulsate around Carter's pumping tongue, and I know I'm close.

My eyes won't leave Brad's. He stands beside me, his hand softly brushing over my shoulder, teasing down to my covered breasts.

"Stop," he says, and Carter stops his attack.

Confusion overtakes the pleasure as Carter lifts me slightly up.

"No," I say, feeling Carter smiling beneath me.

"Sorry, doll, it's Brad's time to play with you." He tosses me away, my arousal drips down his face, and I gulp as he drags it with his fingers to his tongue.

"Don't make me wait too long, Brad. My cock needs to be inside her."

Brad ignores Carter, his eyes never leaving mine. "Take off your clothes, Katie."

Hesitantly, I do as he says. My pussy throbs between my legs. This is the second time tonight I didn't get to climax.

I sit bare on the couch, waiting to see whatever game he's playing.

"Part your legs," he orders as he stands beside Carter, watching me like a hawk.

The bulges in their pants make me inch back. Is tonight the night they will both fuck me?

"Katie," he warns, pulling me back from my thoughts.

I part my legs and watch as they both sit down on the coffee table. Carter shifts in his seat, and I know his control is slipping, but there is nothing on Brad's face to indicate what he's thinking.

"Touch yourself," he says.

I know I can't say no; I know I have to do as he says, but still, I glance at Carter. He gives me a nod, and I take a deep breath.

My fingers trail to my clit, throbbing for attention, and gently rub over it. Pleasure rises as their gazer are locked on my movements.

It feels empowering to have them watching me as I touch myself. Doing what I want. Well, not truly.

My breathing changes, my back arches, and my orgasm is rising. Soft moans spill from my lips as I'm almost there.

Almost—

"Stop."

My moves come to a stop, and I whimper in disappointment.

"You want more, Katie?"

My gaze narrows as Brad taunts me. "Yes."

"Tell me what you are."

What am I? What is that supposed to mean?

I draw a blank, and nothing happens. Nothing other than wetness dripping down, staining the couch.

Carter's impatience is rising; his leg is twitching as his gaze flicks from my dripping pussy to my breasts to my lips.

"I'm just me," I say, unsure what to do.

Brad sighs. "Touch yourself again."

Excitements bubble, and I don't wait another second. My fingers dip between my folds, brushing over my sensitive, needy clit, and I tremble as I rub myself.

My moans are soft and soft; my hips buck in search of more. And my orgasm rises faster than before, my body craving its release.

"Stop."

Are you fucking kidding me? I don't stop. I don't listen.

I'm so close, so close.

Almost.

Fuck.

He rips my hand away and towers over me as my eyes snap to his.

"What are you?"

My chest rises and falls with every breath. My perked nipples brush over his shirt, and I whimper in need. My body and soul crave it all. I need something, anything.

With one hand, he holds my wrists, and his other teases over my heated skin to my stomach and slowly trails lower.

"What are you to us, Katie?"

I yelp as he slaps my sensitive pussy, trying to close my legs, but all I do is cage him in.

He rests the palm of his hand on my clit as his finger teases my entrance.

"Tell me, Katie."

My hips buck on their own; he needs to touch me. Please...

"I'm your slut," I whimper, finally realizing what they want. Carter told me all along.

Brad's lips curve in a smile, and he circles the palm of his hand on my clit. I arch into him, craving more. Anything.

"Now, beg," he whispers.

It snaps something inside me, him telling me to beg.

All that rises is defiance. And even though I know I'll be left with a whimpering pussy, I can't beg. I'll never beg. Not when he smiles at me smugly.

I know he doesn't accept a simple please; he truly wants to see me begging like a needy slut.

I shake my head. My lips pressed firmly together as pleasure coils inside me, clawing to find a way out.

He taunts me, torturing me by bringing me to the edge of my climax, all to stop again.

"Brad." Carter's voice is warming, and I wonder if it's to help me of himself as I'm not the only one affected by it.

"She can't come," he snaps back. "She has to earn it and beg like the good slut she is."

Brad peels himself away from me, and Carter grabs my hair, pulling me from the couch until I'm on my knees before him.

He unzips his pants, mumbling something under his breath as all that escapes me are whimpering moans.

I open my mouth, knowing what's coming. I want it, too; I want him to fuck my mouth senselessly. I want him to use me.

But what I want the most.

I want to come.

Stupid Brad.

# CHAPTER ELEVEN

*Carter*

God, she looks stunning. Her skin is flushed from arousal, and her eyes are filled with lust.

Her pussy drips, waiting for me. But I have to wait. It's Brad's turn, and he likes the torture. He likes to get under their skin, fucking their minds up until they are a begging mess.

He needs control, absolute control.

I do, too, but differently. I take it; I force it.

He does it differently. He scares them. Cares for them, only to be an ass a second later. His mind works twisted. And I love it. I have seen what it does, and I know if I wait for him to continue his plays, I will have the best fuck of my life.

Pre-cum leaks from the tip of my throbbing cock, waiting to be inside Katie. She sits, waiting perfectly still. But the tremble in her legs doesn't go unnoticed. She is on the verge of breaking. Giving the last bit of strength she has left to Brad.

You would think I already took everything from her, but that is why Brad's game works differently. He makes them feel stronger, loved, cared for, and listened to. All to take it away.

To scare them in the dark.

As he did earlier. Assaulting Katie in that alleyway just to get her needy pussy craving to climax.

I should have fucked her before they went away because now my balls are tightening, almost painfully.

One thing I know for sure: if he tells me to stop once I'm on the verge of climaxing, I will punch that stupid grin off his face.

"Wider, doll," I whisper, watching as she listens to me, sticking her tongue out to catch the drop of cum leaking.

She moans, her eyes rolling back, and I give her what she wants. Slowly, I slide inside her, pushing through until I hit the back of her throat. She moves slightly but takes it all.

"You feel so good," I groan as I start to thrust.

Her moans vibrate around my hard shaft, and I feel myself ready to explode. That little show she gives has me on edge, but I don't want to spill my cum just yet. I want to savor this moment because I know Brad isn't going to let me inside her pussy tonight.

A muffled squeal leaves her, and I glance down, noticing Brad kneeling beside her and toying with her cunt.

She squirms and soon rides his hand.

Fuck, that's hot.

My thrust changes, harder and faster, until I hear her gag.

Yes, struggle. Fight me.

She claws at my hip; tears roll down her face as she struggles to breathe.

My grip on her hair tightens, and I shove her face fully against me, feeling my cock slide down her throat as it twitches inside her.

She swallows every drop of cum I give her, and I groan in ecstasy.

And still, I want more. I crave every part of her body.

I pull back my cock and wipe the cum that leaks from her lips over her cheek.

"Our dirty little slut," I mumble.

The corner of her lip twitches as she holds onto me.

Her body tenses, and I know she is ready to climax.

"Beg him, Katie."

She clenches her lips shut and shakes her head. A harsh slap follows, and she screams.

"Beg," I say again as Brad palms her red ass.

And then I see it.

She likes it.

God, she's even more twisted than us two. She wants us to think she isn't. But Brad will teach and show how good we can be to her.

Brad slaps her ass once more, and she moans. A glint of surprise flows through her eyes.

"I won't beg to be allowed to come," she says as her hips buck on his hand.

That will hit a nerve.

Brad rises fast; I inch back as he grabs her wrist, tying them together with his belt. He tosses her over his shoulder, and I notice him inhaling sharply.

Yes, brother, she tastes even more delicious.

He shakes it off and hurries upstairs.

I wonder who will cave first.

Brad or Katie.

I stuff my dick back in my pants and follow them.

The scared little girl vanishes because of Brad. He dares her to be stronger; he likes it that she defies him.

If this all is going to work, and last. We need this.

We need his games.

He needs to train her.

Otherwise, she will run again.

I lean against the doorframe while Brad ties her to her bed. She kicks him and fights. Not enough, though. She never fights hard enough.

He takes it all; the bulge in his pants only grows bigger, and mine is slowly rising again.

Fight, little doll. Fight with everything you have.

"You can sleep on it," he growls, harshly pulling her legs apart. She keeps her lips pressed together, but we can still hear her muffled moan as he plays with her clit.

"You need to learn your place," he warns, pulling his touch away. She whimpers, and he leaves her. As he passes me, he gives me a look in warning.

I nod and walk to Katie. My fingers brush over her skin, and she parts her leg further. Needy little slut. Look how far she has gotten.

"We can't," I say.

"He's an ass," she mumbles.

"Oh, sweet doll, he's just beginning."

# CHAPTER TWELVE

*Katie*

M y shoulder hurts; everything hurts. But what pains me the most is the ache between my legs. The one that never left this entire night.

I couldn't sleep, I couldn't get some rest.

I tried to do something about it, but Brad tied me up too well.

Ass.

And now, as I hear the birds chirping and the morning sun slowly lighting up my room, I hear them.

The door opens, and I hold my breath, aware of how I lay here in the bed. Yesterday, I was high on pleasure. Knowing exactly what I did.

There were no more restraints.

And it felt.

So freeing.

Brad shows himself and edges closer while Carter remains in the doorway. This is as much torture for him as for me.

"Do you want to eat something?" Brad asks, ignoring the fact that I'm naked and tied to the bed.

"Maybe," I mumble with a narrowed gaze.

I never hated him, never thought badly of him. But that has changed.

He laughs softly and sits beside me. "I don't know if I should untie you."

"Why not?"

"You don't behave, you don't listen. You ran away from us yesterday."

I gulp, feeling smaller. They haven't brought it up yet, and now that he does, I feel ashamed. Not even because of the stranger's touch but because I tried to leave them.

I can see the hurt in his eyes, the same one I see in Carter.

"I'm sorry," I whisper. I don't say it to get loose; I say it because I mean it. I never thought I would feel sorry for trying to leave them.

But they are showing me that I'm theirs, which means they are also mine.

"I need more than that, Katie," he says with a tilt of his head.

His hand wanders over my stomach, and something stirs inside me. My legs relax, my pussy wets and I know he can see the reaction my body has to his touch.

I don't want to fight it anymore.

"I won't beg," I say.

A smug smile plasters on his face while I hear Carter curse under his breath.

"You will." His touch leaves me, and he walks out, leaving me tied to the bed.

He says nothing, leaving me alone with Carter.

"Why can't you do as he wants? You are making it very hard on everyone here," Carter says.

He shakes his head and comes closer, untying me.

I rub my hands over my bruised wrists.

"You beg me all the time," he mumbles.

"That's different," I counter, even though I don't know why. Not yet. I will figure it out.

"Go get cleaned up and come downstairs."

I nod as he wanders out of my room.

I'm quick in the bathroom, cleaning myself up. And I can't help it as my fingers brush over my sensitive clit.

Everything inside me screams I shouldn't touch myself, knowing Brad hasn't told me it was okay. But damn, it just hurts.

I lean against the cold tiles; my hand won't listen as I part my legs slightly to let my fingers dip between my legs.

I hiss at the sensitivity as I rub myself. Softly and slowly. My back arches off the wall, and my eyes close as I ride on this thin line of ultimate pleasure.

I feel empty, though. I need more.

The bathroom door opens, and Brad walks inside. My moves stop, our eyes lock, and I see it.

Anger.

I'm frozen on the spot as he strips, ripping his clothes from his body. Heat spreads beneath my skin as my eyes rake over his body.

Shamelessly, I move down until I gulp.

He closes the distance between us and yanks my hand from my clit.

"No," he warns, and I nod.

He's going to kill me with that monster between his legs. I don't have much comparison, but damn.

He cups my pussy harshly and says, "This is mine, you have to earn your climax."

I nod, unable to make words.

"Beg me, Katie. Beg me like the slut you are."

I shake my head and try to push him away.

My defiance still wins over my need to come, but I know it won't remain. Maybe it's stupid that I fight or try. Because I think we all know, I want this as much as them.

He's quick and turns me, slams me against the tiles, and parts my legs.

He rubs his thick cock between my folds. I whimper and struggle as much as I can.

But he doesn't stop, not as he rubs over my entrance, teasing my clit. My lips say no, but my body says yes. My hips tilt back, giving him better access, and I close my eyes.

He doesn't enter me, and my pussy cries. I push back, and the tip slips in. He doesn't move, though. He keeps still and ensures I can't go any further.

"Brad," I moan, on the verge of breaking.

"Beg," he groans and gives me a slight nudge.

My walls stretch around almost painfully. The slight sting quickly disappears as I need more. I need him to fuck me.

"Brad, it hurts."

He pulls slightly out and pushes his tip in again, not giving me anymore.

"Beg," he says again.

My entire body trembles, and I can't hold it. I can't stop it. I have to...

"Please, Brad, please don't stop. I need you to fuck me, please."

He groans loudly, and with that, he slams inside me. I cry out in pain and pleasure as I give him everything he wants.

Giving my soul all I have to give.

Because now, I know.

I'm fully his. I can't go back from this. I can never escape from this.

And I don't want to.

I want more.

I want them to force every desire on me until there is nothing left.

He thrusts me hard. My nipples painfully rub against the tiles, and so does my face as he almost pushes me through the wall.

"You feel so good and tight," he groans behind me as he fucks me harder, his cock hitting the right spot inside me.

I can't hold it; all the teasing and everything he has done pour through me, and tears fall.

"Hold it, don't you dare come."

"I have to," I moan, and my walls clench tightly around his shaft.

He groans, pushing through them.

"Please, Brad, please let me come."

There is this sense of freedom and safety in giving in. A weight lifts off me, and he softly whispers, "I want you to come on my face."

Oh fuck.

My body trembles, my throat runs dry, and I quickly nod.

"Hold on," he groans, fucking through my spasming walls as I hold onto the last remainder of strength I have to not climax.

His thrust slows, quickly pulls out, and turns me, forcing me on my knees.

Spurts of cum paint my face, my mouth open, my tongue catching some drops.

The warm water of the shower washes it away as he pulls me back on my feet, his fingers rubbing over my face, and now I know why Carter did the same yesterday.

"I'm going to paint every inch of your skin with my cum."

I take a shaky breath and nod as he pushes my back against the tiled wall. He lowers himself, lifting my left leg over his shoulder, and then he buries his face between my legs.

My fingers rake through his hair as I pull him closer.

His tongue twirls around my clit, closing in with every breath I take. My hips buck, and he forces them to stop with his hands on my hip.

I push off the wall and scream as he sucks my clit.

A harsh slap on my ass follows, and I moan in pleasure.

"More, please, Brad." All my walls vanish like snow in the sun. I want it all, want it now.

I feel him smile as he attacks my clit, his hand roams to my entrance, and he dips two fingers inside me, pushing to my sweet spot.

I moan and tremble. It's too much, I'm coming.

I have to.

"Please, can I come? I can't stop." I pause, unable to catch my next breath, and then everything breaks.

"Brad!" I scream as my juices spill on his face as he licks me clean.

"Good fucking girl," he groans.

And for the first time since we started our dance, my heart swells. Just the same as Carter says those words.

"I hope you're ready for part two," he teases as he trails kisses up my body.

"Part two?"

"Oh yes, I'm not done with you. And neither is Carter."

# Chapter Thirteen

My body buzzes as Brad leads me to his room. I've never been there, honestly, and I wonder why he's taking me there now.

Is that going to be our room?

Carter waits inside, pacing the room back and forth, and a smile pulls on my lips.

"And?" he asks impatiently, his gaze drifting from mine to Brad.

"Tell him," Brad says, giving me a nudge.

My nerves spike, and I know I shouldn't be nervous. I know they want me; I know that. But now I will be telling them I want them just as much.

Everything, I want it all.

"I'm yours, fully. I won't run, ever."

His eyes glint with excitement. "I still want you to fight me."

"Always," I joke.

Brad tugs me toward him, and he cups my cheek. His thumb brushes over my bottom lip.

"Should we show him what you learned, little slut."

My breath shakes as his eyes are focused on my parted lips.

"Yes," I say.

"Kneel on the bed," Brad whispers, and I hurry.

Carter glances at me with pure lust in his eyes. His fingers hover over my skin as if he is waiting for something.

Even though Brad is the younger one of the two, he seems to be in charge. I don't know why Carter lets him lead; maybe I will never find out.

"She's all yours," Brad says, and Carter doesn't wait another moment.

His touch comes in full need and harshness, as it is always. I whimper as he pushes me back on the bed, harshly spreading my legs. I struggle slightly, and the hunger in his eyes heightens.

"It will only hurt a bit, doll. After that, you will beg us for more. I promise," Carter muses as his fingers dip between my legs, spreading my folds and pushing inside me.

His jaw clenches as if he's trying to control himself. My back arches off the bed as he pumps his fingers inside me.

"Carter," I moan, and his eyes snap to mine. "Hurt me."

A grin teases his lips, and he pulls his fingers out of me. With a harsh grip on my sides, he turns me. He's on me in a second, pressing my face into the mattress until I squirm, fearing I lose my breath.

His cock moves between my ass, and I tilt my hips, desperate to have him inside me. My wall pulsates around nothing, waiting to be filled.

The tip brushes over my entrance, and then he slams inside me. Tears spring in my eyes, and I whimper.

The pain quickly changes as he pulls out and does it again. And again and again until I am a screaming mess.

His thumb pops into my ass, the pressure on my back lessens, and I can breathe fully.

His hand snakes around my throat, and he tilts me up.

"Do you remember what I asked you?"

He adds another finger, stretching me further. I nod as all that falls from my lips are moans.

"Words," he snarls, and I cry as he slams harshly inside me.

"If I wanted to know how good it feels to have you both inside me."

He hums, his pace slowing. "And do you?"

My eyes find Brad, watching us from a distance, a bulge straining his pants. Our gazes lock, and tension crackles between us.

"Yes," I moan, reaching my hand toward Brad.

"Beg me," he says, a smirk tilting on his lips.

Carter pulls out his dick and guides it to my ass. He doesn't wait, and he will never wait or ask. He takes what he wants, and I'm willing to give.

His cock slides inside me, and I bit my lip to keep back the upcoming scream.

"Brad, please, I need you."

Carter groans behind and turns us on our side as Brad rises, ready to join us.

I don't even realize what I asked for; I don't know what it will feel like or that I'm even ready for something like this. But I do know I'm making the choice. Not them.

Carter is holding me tightly, parting my leg further with his free hand as he pumps slowly in my ass.

Brad's heated gaze wanders over my exposed body, his eyes lingering on my perked nipples before they drift down.

He bites his lip and unbuttons his jeans. I hold my breath, knowing what awaits me behind his clothes. My cheeks blush further as his cock jumps free, pre-cum leaking from the tip.

I haven't had him inside my mouth, nothing other than a few drops of his cum, not enough to taste him. Would he taste the same as his brother? Or sweeter?

"Don't worry, you can lick me clean once I'm done destroying you," he muses, noticing my stare.

His dirty words do something to me, and I reach for him, needing him closer.

"Look at that little brother," Carter groans behind me.

"Perfect," Brad teases.

He edges closer, lying down in front of me, and tugs my leg over his hip. I hiss as the tension from Carter's cock increases, but the pain slowly fades as Brad's fingers wander to my clit, toying with it until my orgasm is ready to explode.

"Don't come yet, little slut," Brad warns, his tone harsh, and I gulp with a nod.

I won't get it all if I disobey him; he showed me that. He showed me what it would be like if they only got their fill and left me hanging.

He pushes his cock between my folds, from my clit to my entrance, back and forth as Carter almost stills. He pulls out slightly, and I push back.

"Don't worry, doll. I'm just making some room until you adjust to us both."

I didn't expect this gentle side of him, and it makes me lean back and snake my arm around his neck to tug him closer. His lips hover by the shell of my ear. Every breath and sound that leaves his lips brush over my skin. The closeness feels safe and desired.

Gently, Brad slides his dick inside me, and I pull my lips behind my teeth. Now I understand why Carter was being gentle.

Fuck, this hurts.

I'm a whimpering mess as he slides through until he's completely inside me. I don't dare to breathe; I don't dare to move as I feel on fire.

Lips claim mine, my body melting as my lips follow his lead. Brad kisses me softly, his tongue daring mine to dance.

I never kissed him or Carter.

My moan vibrates around our tongues as his fingers play with my clit. Carefully, Carter pushes deeper, and they both wait inside me for me to tell them I'm okay.

With a slight move of my hips, they start, as I don't want to free my lips from Brad's. Not until I'm forced to.

Carter pulls my head back by my hair, tilting my head in such a way that his lips can claim mine next.

Their pace starts slow, as well as my kiss with Carter. But with every sound, every moan, their pace increases. The fullness is overwhelming, but the pleasure is something I can never put into words.

Pleasure spikes through me; everything feels electric as they move me through this high. I could never get enough of feeling one with them at this moment.

Everything fades, all the worries, all the drama that awaits us, nothing matters.

Only us.

My lips part for Carter, every breath paired with moans while their thrusts change.

The harshness returns, pounding me between them. I can't choose; I don't know which one I crave more. I think I will need them both.

I won't choose.

My walls pulsate, my core tightens, and I know I can't keep it in. I can't stop what's coming.

"Come for us, needy slut," Carter says, and my eyes snap to Brad.

"Come," Brad orders.

My restraints vanish, the storm inside breaks free, and I cry in ecstasy.

Riding through this orgasm that doesn't seem to have an end, not as they fuck me sore, breaking me until they still, spurting their cum inside me. Only then, I fall, fall from the pleasure high.

# Chapter Fourteen

I stir awake; snores from Brad and Carter fill the room, and I squirm myself free from our intertwined bodies.

I can't stop the smile that curves on my lips as, for the first time, I truly feel at peace. There is no fear, no regret.

And I know it will all work out. One way or another.

As I tip-toe to the bathroom, I hear Brad's breathing change. I freeze, not wanting to wake them, and when the sound of his snores continues, I resume my way. My bladder is killing me.

Sitting in silence, my eyes roam around his bathroom. I have never been in here before, but it looks pretty much the same as mine. What lures my attention the most is the black sleeve that hangs out of the laundry basket.

I finish my business on the toilet and quickly wash my hands. My gaze won't leave the sleeve; the thick fabric is too warm for these past few days.

Cautiously, I take it out, and a familiar scent invades my senses.

Cedarwood.

My hands shake as I stuff the thick hoodie back. I inch back, unsure what to do.

It was him; it was Brad in the alleyway. But why? Why he did he do that?

The only explanation that fills my mind is that he's sick and manipulative.

He made me feel safer here, even when he dared me to defy him. He made me feel stronger. A strength I thought I had lost because of Carter.

But now it all feels...

Fake.

As I blink away the tears, I realize I have to get out of the house.

They are still sleeping as I pack a small bag and grab Brad's keys to his truck. I know it's the wrong choice, but taking his car gives me some advantage. At least, that is what I hope as I get in.

Putting the key into the ignition, I realize this will wake them up. Clenching my eyes shut, I turn the key. The truck roars to life, and I quickly take off.

My eyes snap back and forth to the road and the rearview mirror. Even with tears brimming them, I still see my step-brothers running outside, fading into the distance.

I wonder briefly what is going on in their heads. But I won't dwell on it.

Carter might have taken me against my will at first, and I learned to love the way he fucks me, but what Brad did is different. He manipulated me; he betrayed my trust.

Maybe it was a punishment for trying to run from them.

But I rather had him do it while I knew it was him than what I had now. He did it to ensure I wouldn't run anymore, to make me scared of the outside world. To let me think I'm safer inside the house with their cocks inside me.

I'm stupid. I'm naïve for believing this was all okay, what they were doing, what we were doing.

I trusted I was safe with them, but now I see that was all a lie.

I have no idea where I'm going; I have no plan. But I can't trust myself with them around; they will talk out of it, tell me it was just one of Brad's sick desires.

No more.

I thought it was only for pleasure, twisted pleasure, but it feels like more. Somewhere down the line, I started to care for them more than I should have.

My phone rings, Brad's name pops up on my screen, and I reject the call. I'm not ready to talk to him. I don't know if I ever can.

I'm losing. I don't want to listen, but my body screams at me to return to them.

It's because of their tricks; I know it is. I can't give in.

I don't even know why I respond the way I am. Carter did the same thing, but it feels so different. It is different.

The fear I felt in that alleyway wasn't the same as I had with Carter. It was much worse.

My phone won't stop ringing, and I make the mistake of picking it up.

"What?" I ask, trying to hide the tremble in my voice.

"Where are you going? Come home now; it's not safe for you to be alone at night."

There it is, trying to get under my skin again. Manipulating my choices. Toxic ass.

"I think I will be fine if I don't run into you wearing your black hoodie."

A silence follows, and I briefly wonder if he hung up on me.

"Katie, don't test me. Come home," he says.

The hairs on my arms rise, warning me of his threat. But I push it away. He won't find me. I will be safe as long as I keep distance between us.

If I don't see them, they can't persuade me to stay. They can't trick me into being their pet.

I let my urges and pleasure cloud my mind, but not anymore.

"Fuck you, Brad!" I open my window, toss my phone out, and pick up my speed.

Distance is what is going to save me.

I have to believe that.

I have lost track of time, but my eyes are becoming heavy. I have to find a place to crash. I don't even know where I am, and thankfully, I still have a quarter tank of gas.

I take the next exit and try to find a parking lot, or somewhere I can rest for a bit.

Signs of a park show themselves, and I decide to follow them. Ignoring all the horror movies I watched, I park in the empty parking lot and lock the door before crawling into the back seat.

It's not the best option, but I don't have any other choice, do I?

Sleep doesn't take long to take me, and it feels like seconds have only passed when I jump up. Car doors slam closed, and I don't know how I know.

But it's them.

I just know it.

How did they find me?

Leaning up, I peek through the window.

Shit.

Brad is leaning against Carter's car, his arms crossed while wearing that black hoodie. He is staring right at me, taunting me.

I don't see Carter, but I know he's there.

The truck beeps, the doors unlocking. Brad pushed himself off Carter's car, and I don't wait another moment. I leap up and run out the passenger's side.

Straight into Carter's arms.

I drop to the ground, freeing myself from his grip as he curses something under his breath.

Creating as much distance between us, I hear Brad yell, "Run, Katie. And pray I don't catch you."

# CHAPTER FIFTEEN

Running with all I have, I hope the forest is my way out. Hoping it will keep me safe from the ones that chase me.

I hear them closing in. I hear the crumple of leaves beneath their boots becoming louder and louder.

The adrenaline that courses through me is pushing me over my limits, but it isn't enough.

My lungs burn, my muscles follow, and my pace slows.

Tears stream down my cheeks, and I know a hand will grab me.

But it doesn't come.

I don't hear them.

I slow and glance over my shoulder. All I see is darkness.

Coming to a stop, I wonder if I lost them.

I hold my breath, listening to the sounds around me, waiting for a branch to break, a grunt, anything.

All I hear is my own raging heart ringing in my ears.

Releasing my breath, the tension in my body simmers, and a false sense of hope grows.

Perhaps I did lose them?

Should I go back while they search for me here and try to drive off again?

Shaking my head, I decide to take a detour back. I have no idea where they went, but I know they are there.

With every turn, I scan around me, waiting and listening before I dare take another step.

My heartbeat won't slow, still on high alert.

As if it knows I won't win this.

I won't win this.

Whatever this is. Whatever game Brad has been playing.

A branch breaks behind me, and I freeze. Not daring to move an inch.

Until I hear it, his breathing.

He's there.

I clench my eyes shut before I leap forward, but it isn't enough.

It would have never been enough.

I fall to the ground as one of them jumps me. He pushes me to the ground as I fight his hold.

And then, I smell it.

Cedarwood.

His game, his rules.

This is his desire.

"Brad, stop!" I cry out, squirming beneath him.

The same thought as before flows through my mind.

I won't win this.

My clothes are torn from my body until I feel the damp ground on my naked skin.

"You shouldn't have run, Katie. You know what happens if you run."

There is a hint of amusement in his voice. His hard cock pushes through my ass cheeks, ignoring my soreness from earlier because he doesn't care.

He wants to destroy me—my mind and body.

### Brad

She whimpers and fights, as I wanted her to. But I know I already won.

She truly believed I cared for her; I felt it when we kissed. Something changed for her, but she has to be reminded of her place.

My slut.

I thrust inside her. Her pussy wraps around me perfectly, and I don't wait. I fuck her into the ground, taking what is mine.

I hear the sobs, but I know they will change.

They will turn into moans because I know what she needs.

She needs me.

Gripping her hips tightly, I tilt them back, pushing myself deeper and deeper.

Carter shows himself, stepping out of the shadow. Lust and regret joined in his gaze, but his throbbing dick will win.

And it wins.

He pulls down his pants, freeing his cock, and yanks Katie's face from the dirt, guiding his shaft inside her mouth.

I slap her ass as she tries to fight him again and again. The palm of my hand stings, and I know redness paints her skin.

She gives up, her jaw relaxing, and Carter doesn't wait, soothing her with his dirty lines as he pumps his cock inside her.

"Look how pretty you are, doll," he whispers.

Her pussy clenches around me, and I groan.

I could never get enough of her; she feels too good.

She can't hold it back as I slam through her clenched walls, on the verge of an orgasm.

My lips tilt into a smile as I push through. She will come so many times tonight that she will never dare to defy us.

Even though I hope she does.

Tighter and tighter until I still, not daring to spill my cum. Not yet.

She spills hers, squirting all she held back. I don't let her come back from her high and haul her up, forcing her on her knees.

Carter doesn't wait and pulls his dick from her mouth.

"Please stop; I don't want this anymore," she pleads with us.

Her lips tell us to stop, but her body tells us something else.

Pulling out of her, Carter crawls beneath her, taking her pussy as I position myself again.

Fuck, I want us both to be in her cunt.

The thought won't leave me. As Carter pumps inside her, I add my fingers, stretching her.

She screams and begs, and I feel Carter's cock hardening.

I slap her ass again as she tries to move, and she can't control the moan that falls from her lips.

There she is.

"Good girl," Carter sings, and I add another finger as my cock presses at her entrance.

Her body relaxes slightly, giving me enough room to slide beside Carter.

"No, no, stop! Brad, stop!" she cries out.

Carter moves slightly, giving my cock more room before we join our thrust.

She shakes between us, the sensation of us both inside her pussy too much for her to handle.

But I know once the pain fades and the pleasure takes over, she is going to beg us for more.

We slide slowly, picking up our pace with every thrust as we both need more.

She curses, and a soft moan spills.

Carter's hand moves to her clit, adding even more pressure, and I do the same, playing with her ass.

She tenses briefly, but soon, she is overcome with pleasure.

She can't fight it; she can't fight us. Not as we give her all she could ever desire.

"You feel so good, doll," Carter says, his words paired with a groan.

"A perfect slut," I add.

The words push her over the edge, her next orgasm rakes through her, and I struggle with my own.

Stilling briefly, I wait for hers to pass.

Her body is weakening, her legs shaking, and I wrap my arm around her waist, keeping us both up.

"One more," I whisper, and she shakes her head.

"I can't, I can't anymore."

I chuckle and pick up my pace again,

"Oh god, oh god," she cries out.

Carter can't hold it anymore; he tries, but we are both on the verge of exploding.

We push her further, needing one more climax before we can have our own.

We slam inside her, not a rhythm to be found. As animals pounding.

A muffled moan escapes her as her head falls on Carter's chest. Her pussy pulsates rapidly as we both still inside her, our cocks twitching as our cum fills her.

Her body goes limp, and Carter tries to soothe her.

Carefully, I pull out and get dressed as I watch her on top of Carter.

"Don't ever do that again," Carter whispers.

"She won't," I say.

"I wasn't talking about her," he snaps.

He knew my type of games from the start, but he's caring about her more than he should. We were never meant to fall in love with her.

I don't even know if I'm capable of that.

But I know that I'll burn down the world to get to her and hurt anyone who dares to touch what is ours.

Perhaps that is love, at least, my kind of love.

# CHAPTER SIXTEEN

The smile on my lips won't fall as she lies in my arms. Just the two of us as Carter picks up Dad from the airport.

"Don't play games with me," she whispers.

It is something I can't promise as it is what I need, what I desire most.

"Know that I will never do anything to truly hurt you," I say.

She shakes her head and snuggles closer. "But you did."

I know I did; that was why Carter was furious with me, hating what I did to her.

But did he really think it was a coincidence that she found my hoodie?

I chuckle and shake my head; amusement fills me as I have gotten everything that I wanted.

"And still, here you are," I say.

I played my game and twisted her thoughts and mind. Hunted her in the woods and fucked her senseless. I broke her, shattered her, and glued her back together, just as I promised myself I would.

"You can't stay away, Katie," I add.

If I could go back, I would do it differently. I would have made it harder for her. I would have pushed her more.

But we have all the time in the world now.

"I know, but promise me you won't push me away only to punish me after."

She stares at me, her eyes looking for something in mine. She might not realize it yet, but even when the summer comes to an end, I won't let her go. So, I can't promise her that.

I'll be waiting in the shadow to take her how I want.

And all she'll do is beg me for more.

Like the perfect little slut she is.

## Katie

I don't know what I'm doing, but they are like a drug. An addiction I can't get rid of. One I might not want to get rid of.

Carter explained the best he could, telling me about Brad's games and tricks. All that he likes.

If he would have told me sooner, I wouldn't have responded the same. It wouldn't have hurt me so much.

But now I do know.

He can never hurt me like that anymore. He can't twist my thoughts anymore. And I won't be stupid enough to believe he cares.

Carter cares.

I know he does.

And Brad, I don't know if he's capable of caring.

Not after what I have seen.

Or maybe this is his way of caring.

Anyway, everything will be different.

Because their father is coming home. I don't really know why Mom isn't coming with him. Maybe he knows something is up between us three.

I don't think this is my happy ending in all this. Maybe there isn't one. Maybe I should just enjoy the ride while it lasts. Enjoy all the desires they force on me.

Or perhaps there is more...

# CHAPTER SEVENTEEN

I have no idea what is going on as Carter and Brad have been in Henry's, their father's, study for the last hours.

My stepfather didn't even look at me when he came inside and went straight for Brad.

Did he find out what happened between us three?

Is he going to do something about it?

But...

Do I even want it to stop?

I smile as I shake my head. I don't.

Not anymore.

I'm no longer afraid, and I crave every bit of them.

My thighs rub together as images fill my mind, reminding me how they call me their little slut and force everything they have on me. But can I still say force as I like to fight back? Craving it as much as them...

Fuck, I'm so messed up.

It's just two more weeks, and then I go back to college. And all this will be a dirty dream to keep me company.

The office door creaks open, and Carter steps out, heading straight upstairs without even a glance at me.

My curiosity is winning, and I quickly follow behind him. I hear him cursing and tossing stuff through his room. I peek inside. Clothes fly across the room, landing on the suitcase on his bed.

No, what's happening? He can't leave me.

"What are you doing?" My eyes sting as tears threaten to spill; he doesn't look at me, pretending I don't exist.

"Carter?" Still nothing.

I'm invisible as he continues to pack.

My jaw sets as I lock the door behind me and slowly peel my dress from my skin, leaving me in just my bra and panties.

"You're not leaving me," I whisper, edging closer.

His body tenses, his moves slow, and my eyes snap to his pants as I moisten my lips, watching his cock strain his pants.

"You belong with me." My fingers brush over his hand, trailing higher to take off his shirt. "In me."

"Katie, stop."

"Why should I listen? You never did."

He grabs my wrist; anger and pain fill his eyes as his jaw ticks. "I knew what you wanted, what you needed."

"What do I want now? Need now?" I dare him, stepping closer, my knee moving between his legs.

"Our father—"

"Yours, he's not mine."

"What he want—"

"I don't care, Carter." I don't want to hear it; I don't need excuses. Right now, I don't even care what happened downstairs, not as my pussy throbs in need, soaking my panties.

His gaze rakes over my body as he bites his bottom lip. "You have to be quiet." The corner of his lip lifts.

I tilt my head, rubbing my leg against his hard cock. "I will try."

"On the bed, ass up," he orders.

"*Make* me."

There he is.

The fire in his eyes, the need to take me. Truly fuck me like the animal he is.

His grip on my wrists tightens as he hauls me to the bed. I struggle slightly, pulling back, and he groans, enjoying the play.

He fists my hair, tilting my head back as his lips hover over mine.

"What are you?" he asks.

I grin. "Your little slut."

He guides my hand to his strained cock, rubbing himself with my hand. "Feel what you're doing to me."

I yelp as he moves quickly, tossing me on the bed and ripping my panties from my heated skin.

"Who said you could wear this?" he sneers, slapping my ass in punishment, my pussy dripping.

My body quivers at the faint sound of his zipper being undone, and I part my legs slightly and curve my back.

"So needy," he says, chuckling, lining his cock against my entrance, rubbing the head through my wetness.

I inch back, feeling the tip slide inside, and moan as he pushes further.

"Don't make a sound," he warns and thrusts deeper, stilling a moment. I bury my face into the mattress, muffling my whimpers as he pulls back and slams inside, his balls slapping against my clit.

My moans are muffled as I move my hips back as he slams forward. I know I should fight more, but fuck, this feels good.

His hand snakes around my hip as he leans over me. His fingers play with my clit as his warm breath fans over my ear.

Sweat coats our bodies as I climb higher. My pussy clenches around his cock, and he groans loudly.

"Fuck, come for me, little slut." He pinches my clit, and I scream. My body twitches beneath him, and my pussy spasms as I squirt.

"Good fucking girl," he muses as his fingers leave my oversensitive clit.

A loud banging on the door erupts, and panic courses through me. Carter curses, his movements stop, and we both stare at the door.

"I locked it," I whisper, but Carter shakes his head as we hear the lock turn.

The door flings open, and my stepfather's eyes widen as he takes in the scene. I don't know what to do as I stay completely still.

He moves fast, grabbing Carter and tossing him off me. I crawl up the bed and curl in a ball.

"Downstairs! NOW!" he roars and stomps out of the room.

Brad watches us from the doorway, leaning against the frame with his arms crossed.

He doesn't say anything as Carter scampers up and pulls up his pants. I'm still sitting on the bed, unmoving as a deer staring at headlights closing in.

Knowing you're fucked.

I put on the same dress as before, trying to clean my pussy as my thighs glisten with my own arousal.

"Now, Katie!" Brad grabs me, pulling me out of Carter's room.

"I'm not wearing any—"

"It doesn't matter," he snaps as we head downstairs to the living room.

My stepfather paces in front of the couch, mumbling to himself. The table in front of the couch is missing, shoved to the side, and my brows pinch.

Brad pushes me to his father, and I don't dare to look up as he stares down at me.

"You let them fuck you?"

Let them?

No.

Maybe.

Yes.

"They are your brothers!"

"*Step*brothers," I quickly say, as if that will make it better.

"Look at me," he snaps.

I gulp, peeking up, meeting his dark blue eyes. His hair was a grayish color, just like his beard. His brows set in a deep frown.

"You want them to fuck you?" he pauses, his gaze shifting between Brad and Carter. "Both of them?"

# CHAPTER EIGHTEEN

I silently nod, not daring to look away.

"How does it feel?" my stepdad asks.

My lips part, but no words follow; I blink a few times, wondering if I heard it right.

His jaw ticks, and his patience is thinning.

"Good, it feels good."

"Do you like their cocks?"

I don't know where this is going. As I inch back, his hand collars my throat, keeping me in place.

"Answer me!"

"Ye-yes," I stammer.

His grips loosen slightly, but he doesn't let me go as his gaze travels lower. "How does she feel?"

"Fucking perfect," Brad answers.

"This is wr—" He doesn't finish his sentence and pushes me down. "On your knees. Filthy whore."

I try to stay on my feet, but he's too strong as he pushes me down to the ground.

"Your mother will have a heart attack when she hears," he mumbles, and a smile I have seen before curls on his lips.

The same smile his sons have when they give in to their lusts and desires.

My body shakes as he rubs his thumb over my lips. "Did you ever have three cocks at once?"

"Dad plea—"

"Shut it, Carter. You two turned her into your personal slut, trained her how I taught you, and now I'm here to put it to the test."

He forces my mouth open and pushes his finger inside. "Suck it, whore," he orders.

My lips wrap around his finger as tears prickle my eyes.

"I waited for this ever since I first saw you, my little angel, born to be my whore. And then my sons had to grab you first." He shakes his head as he unzips his pants with his other hand.

"When you turned sixteen, I couldn't hold it anymore. I couldn't have you sitting on my lap with that tight ass of yours with my cock as hard as steel."

A tear rolls down my cheek as my body shivers. His thick hard cock springs free, and I inch back, releasing his finger with a pop, pleading with Brad and Carter as my gaze shifts between them.

Carter's jaw ticks, his arms crossed as he looks behind me at the wall, pretending this isn't happening. But Brad, Brad enjoys it.

I see the grin, that evil glint in his eyes, and the big bulge in his pants.

"But now I will have you, every fucking hole."

"Please don't. I'll behave. I promise," I plea, but as with his sons, he doesn't hear it. Doesn't care for it.

"I will fuck you in your sleep, I will fuck you in the grocery store, and when you beg me to stop..." His lips curve and a dark laugh. "Don't make me punish you."

He grabs my chin, forcing me to open my mouth as he sharply thrust his cock inside. My jaw stings as he pushes through, the tip gliding further as I gag around it.

His fingers intertwine with my hair, keeping me still.

He groans loudly, my sight blurs as tears fill them, and then he starts pumping his cock inside my mouth as I try to breathe through my nose. It's messy, it's rough, saliva drips off my chin, tears roll, and he only groans in pleasure.

"Rip her dress off," he orders, and I squirm, trying to see who is coming closer. A cold hand brushes over my neck, and I whimper, recognizing his touch.

Brad.

He kneels down as he tilts his head closer. "I wonder, if I dip my fingers in your cunt how wet you are."

I clench my thighs together as the fabric is torn from my body, leaving me naked and bare for my stepfather while he punishes me with his cock deep down my throat.

My stepfather inhales sharply, and my eyes snap up, watching his drift over my heated skin, licking his lip as he keeps my head between his hands.

"How wet is she?" he asks.

Brad chuckles, his fingers graze over my hip, and I hate what surfaces, how I respond to his touch, how he taught me to crave everything he does to me. Knowing, if I'm good, he will give me everything.

His fingers dip between my legs, and as he teases gently on my clit, my thighs relax, and pleasure rakes through me.

He moves further, curling his finger and thrusting it inside me. "She's dripping, Dad."

"Fuck." His movements slow, his grip on my hair tightens, and I whimper. "I want to see all our cum in that pretty mouth of yours."

Brad doesn't wait, rising to his feet and freeing his strained cock. He grins, stroking himself as precum leaks from the tip.

"Carter, you too!"

His steps are slow as he stands on my other side, a gaze I can't decipher, almost as if he's pitying me. Since when does he care?

"Touch yourself. Come with us," Brad orders, and the thick cock leaves my mouth.

My eyes are wide as I stare at the three men towering over me, cocks leaking, hard as steel.

"I-I I don't know, I—" My words are stammers; my thoughts are a mess.

"Don't think, little angel. Be yourself, the dirty slut that lives inside you. Let her out to play," my stepdad muses.

My face is a mess, hair sticking to my wet cheeks and chin, wet from the tears and saliva. And yet, they look at me with such hunger in their eyes, as if I'm all they desire.

"Be my little whore." My stepdad brushes his fingers over my chin. An act that is gentle and caring, and my heart swells. This *need* to be good, to make them proud, surfaces, and my pussy drips, betraying my dirtiest ideas.

Brad grins. "And my dirty slut."

My gaze snaps to Carter as he stays quiet. "Carter?"

"You're all I want, doll, and you're doing so good," he praises.

A soft smile curves as I lick my bottom lip. My gaze shift between the three cocks above me. They all seem the same length but have different thicknesses. My stepdad is winning by far, making me wonder if I can take it.

My fingers graze over my heated skin, brushing over my perked nipples and trailing lower. Brad groans, and my stomach tightens in response.

I softly moan as my hips buck against my hand, my wetness coats my skin, and my face heats at how wet I am.

"Fuck, I can hear how wet your tight little pussy is," my stepfather says while pumping his cock faster and orders. "Finger yourself."

I glance at Carter, and he softly nods, giving me that gentle push I need from him.

"Come on, don't be shy now," Brad jeers.

I let out a soft moan as my fingers thrust inside my pussy. Then I lean forward, licking over my stepdad's hard cock, tasting the salty pre-cum.

He lets out a throaty groan, and then I move to Brad, licking and sucking the head of his cock as my fingers work inside me.

My moans vibrated around his cock, and he hisses. My lips curve as much as they can, knowing he can come at any second.

I release his dick with a pop and edge closer to Carter.

With my eyes locked on his, I let his cock glide in my mouth, taking him as deep as possible. His free hand rakes through my hair, tugging me even closer as all I can do is swallow.

"Show me why they keep fucking you no matter how wrong it is," my stepdad orders sharply.

Obediently, I work harder, moaning for them, licking the heads of their cocks to flash my tongue. I don't hide how good my fingers make me feel.

I know I want them. I want them to keep looking at me like they're incapable of wanting anything or anyone else.

"Open your naughty mouth, dirty little whore," my stepfather commands.

I obey without question, opening my mouth wide and sticking out my tongue.

Brad groans and bursts first, his cum raining down on me in hot spurts, covering my cheek, my temple, and my lips. I lick at the salty fluid eagerly as I moan and tremble. I'm so close to coming.

"She's so fucking eager," my stepdad groans, watching me as his stomach tightens and he increases the pace of his dick.

"Of course, she is," Brad says, crouching down beside me and letting his fingers roam over my body.

"Keep touching yourself," Carter adds as Brad toys with my clit.

I'm panting, and moaning as Brad's cum rolls over my face, dripping from my chin and my breast.

I'm so close, right there on the edge. I can't keep myself quiet anymore. "Please! I want more."

I can't believe what I'm saying, but my orgasm is on the brink of crashing through me.

"So greedy for cum, aren't you?" my stepdad snarls.

I glance at Carter, and he nods again. I shouldn't stop. I don't want to stop. I want them to coat my face in their cum, marking me as theirs to use, marking me as their own personal whore, slut, and doll. Whatever they call me, I take.

Carter comes next, his cum splashing across my face. I close my eyes and part my lips as I savor the taste.

"Good girl," he praises, as his thumb brushes over my cheek.

My stepfather is next, and he comes with a loud groan. His cum drenches my hair, my cheeks, and my chin.

This is so dirty, so wrong, and with that thought, electricity rushes through me, my pussy spasming around my fingers as Brad pinches my clit.

A soft whisper brushes over my ear, his command raking through me. "Come."

My thighs slicken as my juices squirt out; I cup my breast with my other hand, slick with their cum, and I jerk on my nipple, wanting to ride out this pleasure as long as possible.

"Now show me what a good slut you are. What are you going to do with that mess?" my stepdad asks.

My fingers, coated in their cum, graze up to my lips. He watches me closely as my lips curve. Knowing what his *desire* is.

I stick out my tongue, rubbing my fingers one by one over it, savoring their mixed cum with a soft moan.

Brad moans. "So fucking good."

"Our obedient little slut," Carter muses.

My stepfather smirks. "Even better than I expected."

They definitely have me all fucked up, dirty, slutty, so desperate to try all the naughty things they can think of.

And somehow, I like it more than I ever thought I would.

# Chapter Nineteen

## *Henry*

Sleeping like the angel she is, all a mask for what she is beneath the surface. My cock is hard as steel, and I stroke it as I peel the flimsy sheet from Katie's body.

I groan as she lays there with only her panties on, her breasts free for the taking. I lean closer, popping a nipple in my mouth, sucking harder until it's a hard tip, and then move over to the other.

Carefully, I crawl between her legs while I continue teasing her nipples with my tongue.

She stirs slightly, and a soft moan falls from her parted lips, as I nudge her panties to the side, rubbing my cock over her pussy, coating it with her wetness.

She stirs again as I tease her clit; her hand brushes lower as she senses this need for more snakes under it.

I dip my cock, slowly pushing inside as she tries to move away; my grip on her tightens.

"Shh, go back to sleep," I whisper, thrusting inside her.

She makes a soft sound, but her eyes remain closed as her head turns to the other side.

I thrust deeper, taking my time, drawing back, then giving her another inch as her legs twitch and her fingers curl.

She's beautiful, always has been, and looks so damn innocent except when she gives me that knowing look. The one that says she wants every dirty fantasy I can offer.

I stop as her body tenses, waiting for her to look at me, wondering if she would scream or fight me.

Or would she pull me closer?

After a moment, she goes mostly limp again. Asleep, as if nothing is happening, as if this is a secret for me, and only me.

I sit up on my knees slightly, pushing her legs wider, wanting to see how my cock impales her, how her wetness soaks me.

As I draw back, my wet cock moves out of her before disappearing into her wet pussy again.

She shifts and squirms a little, but I'm not stopping until *I* want to.

My control is slipping; I brace my hands on the inside of her thighs as I increase the pace. Her legs quiver, and her lips part.

"That's right. It's just a good dirty dream," I hum. "Being Daddy's little whore."

Her breath catches when I slam inside her. She moans softly, her hips lifting slightly. I smirk. She's going to dream about me fucking her. Going to crave it until she's as bold as she is with Carter and Brad.

Katie won't be able to keep hiding her naughty, slutty side.

She's twitching, moaning, arching, and right on the edge of waking up, and I stop again. Fuck, she's killing me.

I can't get the image of this afternoon out of my mind, how my cum moved over her tongue, how it painted her breasts, and now I want to know how it looks as it drips from her tight cunt.

My arms shake on her thighs, watching her closely, how her breath steadies. The tension in her spine fades, and I let go.

I barrel into her, taking all I want from my little whore. Her pussy grips me hard, her body ready to explode.

Her bed squeaks, and the headboard slams against the wall. Her eyes move beneath the lids, and Katie squirms again.

"Back to sleep. Enjoy your dreams, lose yourself in them," I chuckle.

She makes a soft sound, but her eyes don't open again. I know she needs this. She knows it, too. She craves our attention, our touch, and everything else we can teach her.

I give up on restraint. I fuck her hard, fast, relentlessly, loving how wrong this is, loving the soft, breathy sounds she makes against my hand. I'm so close, right there, right at the edge of ecstasy, when a door slams shut somewhere in the house.

Freezing, I wait to hear footsteps, wait for Katie's bedroom door to open.

It doesn't.

After a few seconds, I move in with Katie again. Potentially being caught makes my slow, even strokes so much more intense. Anyone catching me fucking my step-daughter while she's asleep... fuck, the turn-on.

Even though I know the only two who can catch me are my sons, the ones who have been enjoying Katie for too long.

I groan and lick over her nipple again, sucking the hard peak until I'm on the edge of coming.

My cock hardens, growing bigger inside her as I still, my cum spurting out, filling her. I'm panting, sweat drips from my skin, and I gently pull out. Leaning back, I part her pussy to see how my cum leaks from her cunt.

Fucking perfection.

I don't wipe her clean as I want her to know who fucked her in her sleep. I take her hand, plunging her fingers inside her, coating them with our juices, and place it on her lips.

She moves, her lips part, and I push the fingers inside her mouth.

"Don't we taste good together," I whisper, putting her fingers in my mouth next.

I grab my boxers and slide them on before leaving her alone. As I close the door behind me, Carter waits for me. Leaning against the wall with his arms crossed.

"You couldn't wait anymore?" he asks, a grin plastered on his face.

"Just like you." I smile and pat his shoulder as I head to my bedroom.

"When is her mother coming back?"

I freeze, rubbing the palm of my hand over my face. "She won't be back any time soon, and she will probably even miss sending Katie back to college."

"And then, what happens next?"

"What do you mean?"

"I can't stop. I don't even want to go back to London."

There it is, the thing I feared. Carter was always the softest one of us three. But I have to be honest, I don't blame him.

How can one ever get enough of Katie?

"And then what? Are you going to creep around her dorm when she goes back to Harvard?" I chuckle, shaking my head.

"No, I kn—"

"Carter, she is a good fuck, a really good fuck. But that's it."

"Right." He shakes his head, pushing himself off the wall as he saunters to his room.

This is why I sent him away. I saw it then, and I see it now. He likes her, truly likes her. He has feelings he shouldn't have.

I hoped the time apart would do him some good, but it seems his feelings for her have only grown.

I don't know what that would do with our situation. As every girl, Katie surely wants to have a family of her own, but I can't give her that.

But can I see her with someone else? Someone who isn't one of my sons?

## Katie

My legs stick together as I wake, the smell of sex and cum fills my nose, and my eyes flutter open. Tossing the sheet off my body, I gasp. Red markings cover my nipples, and dried cum paints my thighs.

Oh my god.

He did it.

He fucked me while I was asleep.

I shake my head and get out, needing to scrub my body clean. But as the thought comes to an end, I freeze.

Is that all I think?

All I care about?

What about my stepfather fucking me?

Nothing comes as I wait for the panic to consume me.

It doesn't rise; something else does.

My clit prickles, my core tightness, and I gulp as I feel myself becoming wetter.

Even as my heart stammers, my skin reddens, my pussy whimpers.

Fuck.

I'm so screwed.

# CHAPTER TWENTY

Both Carter and Brad have their own kinks and desires, but it seems they all got it from their dad as I walk through the grocery store, pushing the cart, sensing someone is watching me.

Just like he warned me and said he would fuck me during my errand. My cheeks heat, my pussy throbs in anticipation as I like all their games, even the ones I shouldn't.

There is something different. Something has shifted.

I play along.

I don't fight, I drown.

I don't run, I wait.

I don't hide, I beg.

Even now, as my fingers skim the vegetables, searching for the prettiest, I want it.

Everything.

And maybe even more.

Every step I take, he comes closer. Every corner I turn, he follows.

And it's not until we arrive at the canned food aisle that he touches me.

"Look what I found," he whispers as he leans closer; his body wraps around me, and I inch back.

Will he touch me here? Or will he take me to the bathroom and then use me there? Or he could take me to an employee-only area and actually fuck me.

"What did you find, Daddy?" I taunt, eager to know what he does next.

"My little whore, hungry."

I hum, tilting my hips back. He already fucked me once when I was asleep, the dried cum on my body when I woke up was proof of that, and the thought made my legs tremble, my core tightening as my clit pulsated in need, wondering if I came.

"Do you want Daddy's cock, right here where anyone can find us?"

My face heats as I gulp, and yet, I say, "Please," and part my legs, feeling his hand move under my dress, trailing higher until he dips his fingers inside me. I squirm against him, my ass brushing his hard cock as he teases me with his fingers.

"Fuck, you're dripping," he groans and fumbles with his belt and zipper. "Hold on to the shelf."

I do as he says and stand on my toes as he moves lower. I don't even look around, not caring if anyone sees because all I want is his cock inside me, pounding until I'm a shattered mess.

His mess.

"You love this, don't you? You love being used for my pleasure. You love being touched even though you know anyone could see us," he groans.

My head falls back on his chest, his grip on my hips tightens as he thrusts inside me. Pleasure rakes through me, my stomach tightening and my legs trembling as he moans in my ear. Whispers follow and praises fall.

"Look at how good you're taking Daddy's cock. Such a good whore."

I moan, my pussy quivers around his cock, and he groans again.

"If you keep squeezing me like that, I won't last very long."

He tilts his hip, hitting me harder as I see movement from the corner of my eye. Daddy sees it, too, as he curves his body over mine, giving the impression we are tightly hugging, at least if you don't look too long.

His hand snakes forward, cupping my mount as he toys with my clit. "Come with me." His voice is low as he whispers in my ear.

He leans slightly back, gazing around, as he pounds inside me, our bodies slapping together.

"I will wait in the car," he says and gives me a soft peck on the cheek.

I hum, pretending nothing has happened, and pick up a can as I see an employee storming my way, reading the ingredients of the back while the old woman looks at me suspiciously. There is nothing to see, not anymore, but I feel Daddy's cum drip down my thighs. Lower and lower.

And I know once I move and walk to the check out, everyone can see.

The old woman gives me one last look before she leaves me, and I quickly walk to the register.

Thank god there is no one behind me as I feel the moisture on my dress.

With a polite smile, I pay for the groceries, stuff them in a bag, and head outside without even daring to look over my shoulder as I hear some whispers.

Brad's pick-up truck awaits me as I step outside. The cold evening breeze cools my flustered skin, and I meet my stepdad's gaze as he leans against the truck. His arms crossed, the corner of his lips curve slightly, and I can't help the small surge I feel in my clit.

He pushes off the truck and opens the door for me, and as I get in, my dress inches up enough for him to get a glimpse of the cum that drips from my pussy.

He pushes me forward, and I yelp. "Look how pretty," he muses as I glance up at Brad behind the wheel.

My stepdad thrust his fingers inside me, and I softly moan. Brad edges closer; his hand brushes over my cheek while his other unzips his pants.

My eyes snap down, knowing what will happen next.

My stepdad shifts behind me, shielding me from prying eyes as Brad pumps his hard cock. I lick my lips, trying to inch closer as my body tightens with pleasure.

"Look at that, so eager for another cock," my stepdad groans.

My fingers trail closer as Brad releases his cock. The cold evening breeze brushes over my bare ass as my stepfather taps his fingers over it. Waiting, teasing as my pussy clenches, hating how close his fingers feel, but never giving me what I need—crave.

Fuck, I'm broken. A broken mess, desperate for another orgasm.

And yet, there is this tingle in the back of my head, luring me closer, eager to know what kind of punishment Daddy has for me when I misbehave. I know Carter will fuck me until I can't breathe; Brad messes up my mind until my heart cracks.

But my stepdad... I have no clue.

But I'm sure I will find out.

As I try to crawl closer to Brad, licking my lips as I know how he tastes on my tongue, a harsh slap on my pussy follows. I whimper, glancing over my shoulder as my skin stings.

"Don't move," he orders, and his head dips lower. "Let me clean my little whore up." His warm breath fans over my skin, and his lips brush closer to my dripping pussy, to the mess he created earlier.

My cheeks redden, and I gasp as his tongue plunges inside me.

"Oh go—" My words cut off as Brad grabs my face, forcing me to look at him as he guides his cock in my mouth.

"Shhh now," he whispers. "Make me remember how good you can be for me."

There is something different; I can see it in his dark gaze. I can see the lust and need, but there is more—something I haven't seen before, at least not with him.

I have seen it with Carter, this small glint. One I don't recognize.

Brad's fingers intertwine with my hair as he tugs me closer; I move slightly and whimper as Daddy sucks harshly on my clit in a warning.

Brad chuckles, pushing his cock deeper, and I suck harder as heat courses under my skin, my body shaking.

"I don't like when you leave me," Brad whispers, and my brows knit. Is this why he went with us? Even though his dad said that he didn't need to.

I blink away the thought as I struggle to breathe, his cock buried deep down my throat as my stepdad licks me clean.

I know I shouldn't let it get to me, not daring to think he cares because the last time I went there, he broke a piece of me.

A piece I don't think will heal again.

# Chapter Twenty-One

I shouldn't be doing this; this is wrong.

Too wrong.

But, I... I want to.

Is it still bad if I want to do what he did to me? Touching him as he sleeps, taking pleasure from him how I want, not because he gives it to me.

Pushing the door open, I peek inside. The lights from the street give me enough to see. His soft snores echo through the room, and I tip-toe inside, closing the door behind me.

Trying to control my breathing and raging heart, I fail. My hands shake as I edge closer, and my breath quivers as I see him sleeping only in his boxers.

The flimsy sheet only covers one of his legs and a part of his boxers, but nothing more. I sneak into his bed, every move slower than the one before, as I listen closely to his snores.

Doubt lingers in the back of my head, and I struggle to push it down.

I never took charge like this, and it makes me hesitant.

Crawling over his bulky body, my fingers brushing through his chest hair, my lips gently follow as I snake lower.

With the palm of my hand, I rub over his covered cock, feeling it harden beneath my touch.

I grin, enjoying my new, daring side.

After that moment downstairs, when they painted my skin with their cum, claiming me as theirs, something changed.

I think now, I have all I wanted with my dirty thoughts, the dreams changing into reality. It might have started with Carter, but that was never enough.

I wanted them all.

With that in mind, I trail to his cock, pulling it out of his boxers and slowly stroke him. The lingering doubt fades until there is only excitement, and this need to feel him inside me takes over.

He stirs slightly, and I hold my breath, not daring to make a sound as I continue my pumping touch.

I lean closer, my lips grazing over the pre-cum that leaks from his tip. Cautiously, I press down until my lips part, wrapping around the head. I move further, letting his cock glide inside my mouth until I hit the back of my throat.

I swallow, and my muscles work around him, tugging him deeper until my nose is nudged against his pelvis.

My clit pulsates in need, and I rub my thighs together as I bob my head. Gliding his cock in and out of my mouth as my cheek hollow, building pressure.

His cock hardens further, and I hear him groan. The sound vibrates through me, and my back arches in response.

I lick and moan, my tongue teasing his balls and then running up his shaft, savoring every inch of him.

Shifting beside him, as my pussy weeps for attention, I crawl over him, my legs on either side of his hips, the head of his cock teases between my legs, and I suck in a breath as I guide it to my entrance, needing to feel him inside.

I might have started as a play, doing what he did to me, but god, am I turned on right now—being in total control, doing all what I want—taking the pleasure I want.

And yet, I'm hesitant as he slides inside me.

I blink, the realization hitting me hard as I truly see what I'm doing.

Trying to ride my stepdad.

Strong hands wrap around my hip. "Take what you want, my sweet angel."

I find him staring at me, the corner of his lip tugged into a smile, and my heart swells as he calls me his sweet angel.

I want to be both the dirty whore he uses and his angel.

Pushing down further, I gasp as my walls wrap around him, pulling him in. I inch up, feeling his cock glides out of me, and then I move down again.

I start slow, unable to look away from his burning gaze. My hips tilt with every move, and he lets me lead.

This is bad, too bad to speak out loud, but it feels so *so* good.

I lean forward, just slightly, as my fingers rake over his chest. He tilts his head back as my fingers sweep over his throat.

"Take everything you want, angel. I'm all yours now."

*Angel.* There it is again.

"Not your whore?" I taunt, my fingers curling around his throat, my heart stammers, my pussy throbbing around his cock as my pace increases.

"You are, when I fuck you like you deserve but now," he pauses, slightly lifting my hips as he thrusts with me.

"You're my sweet angel, taking what you want. Just perfect."

Tears prickle my eyes as it falls into place what I mean to him, what he wants from me. He wants to fuck me senseless, punish me, force me into doing his bidding like a whore, but he also craves this, me taking what I want. I'm not the whore who begs now. Now, I'm the one who doesn't wait.

I take.

I squeeze harder, and he grins at me.

"I'm coming, Daddy," I moan, my body shaking, sweat dripping down my spine, and I hear the door softly creak open.

He groans beneath me as my pussy spasms, my body twitching as my juices squirt out, covering him. My grip falters, and I fall on top of him.

Eyes becoming heavy as his dick softens, I whisper, "Can I stay?"

His arms curl around me, holding me close. "It seems someone is missing you."

I hum, snuggling closer as I hear him talking again. The voices sound farther and farther until nothing is luring me awake.

Something feels sticky between my legs as I turn in bed. Without opening my eyes, I dip my hand between them and chuckle as I feel what it is.

Cum. Daddy's cum.

I smile as I remember what I did and slowly open my eyes. There is no one beside me, but I don't feel alone.

I sit up, rubbing my eyes, and there he is.

My monster, Brad, lurking from the corner of the room.

"You never did that with me," he says, his arms crossed over his bare chest.

"Sleep with you? Yes, I did." I wrap the sheets around me tighter as goosebumps rise on my skin.

He stalks closer and yanks the sheet from my body. I gasp as a chill runs up my spine.

"Don't hide from me," he snaps as his jaw ticks.

I sigh, extending my hand to him. "Come."

He remains rooted on the spot; the corner of my lips lifts slightly. "Please," I add, he hesitantly takes it and crawls in beside me as his gaze travels over my naked skin.

I was right when I thought something had changed for him. But he isn't the only one who has grown, changed, accepted, and loved all that's happening.

"What is it?" I ask, even though I know it's a question he might not have the answer to.

"I like sharing you." His words make my brows knit, as I don't get how he sees that as an answer.

"But?"

"I don't know." He shrugs and gets from the bed, leaving me even more confused than before.

I thought I lost the confusion about my situation, how wrong it was to feel okay with all this, with needing all this. And even the turmoil of how I truly wanted it, yes or no.

To finally see some clarity, feeling like I got some say, some control. I showed that last night.

And yet, now, as Brad storms away from me, I'm even more confused than before.

Shaking my head, I get out and stroll into the bathroom of my stepdad. As I glance in the mirror, I laugh; my face is a mess, and my hair is sticking out in all the wrong places, but what surprises me is the happiness in my eyes that I haven't seen in a long time—this glow I don't recognize on myself.

I'm quick with my shower and try to look my best. No one disturbs me, and I can't help but feel that same disappointment again—the one I had when Carter wasn't waiting for me.

It's weird, I know. I don't even know why my mind works like this, why I depend on them so much. Need them for every second.

# CHAPTER TWENTY-TWO

I don't want to say it; I don't want to think it. But I miss him. I miss Carter. With Daddy's plays and Brad trying to squirm himself in it.

I miss my big step-brother. I know he wanted to leave, but I never asked him why. Maybe he just wanted to run, but the thought of him leaving me makes this sharp sting emerge.

Would he leave me?

The sound of his voice lures me to Dad's office. I listen in, realizing he's probably on the phone. Surely, his work must be wondering when he's coming back.

There is only one week of summer left, and then... this all... disappears.

The door is slightly open, enough for me to sneak through. My lips curve as I bend down, crawling through the crack. Carter's voice doesn't change as I hear him type on his laptop.

"... A few more days..." I hear him say, and I clench my eyes shut.

I'm right, he's leaving.

What was I even thinking? I still have to go back to college, and Carter doesn't even live here; he has to go back to London at some point.

I shake my head, forcing the thoughts from my mind, and continue my crawl.

I will remind him he shouldn't leave me.

He needs me, just as I need him.

I move under the desk, noticing the slight twitch in his leg, a nervous tell he has. His legs part, and I edge between them, not touching him, not yet.

I peek up, knowing he could see me, as I run my hands over his legs. He flinches and curses under his breath as he tries to roll back in his chair.

My grip on his legs keeps him in place, and his eyes snap down. The panic disappears quickly, and a grin spreads on his face.

"...yeah, yes, I'm still here," he hastily says.

My fingers trail to his zipper, watching as it becomes strained. I lick my lips, opening his pants and zipper. I tug it down, taking his boxer with it, freeing what waits for me underneath.

He shifts in his seat and talks through his phone as I take his hard cock in my hands. He leans back as I stroke his cock, teasing the tip with my tongue.

He groans softly, and I wrap my lips around the head, swirling my tongue over it.

"Greg, I have to call you back," he says as I sharply suck.

He tosses the phone to the side, his fingers rake through my hair, tugging me closer.

"You missed me that much?" he taunts, and I hum. "Fuck, we shouldn't do this here, dad will get mad if we do. And I'm sure I will not be the one punished."

I shrug my shoulders, and suck harder. Embracing my daring side as I wonder what Daddy will do to me. My thighs rub together as excitement rises.

He hisses, his hip moving up. "Good girl," he praises, and my heart swells, and my pussy clenches.

I move faster as he pants, thrusting his hips up as he forces me to go deeper and deeper.

Struggling for air, he suddenly pinches my nose, and I slap his legs.

"Oh, no. Don't forget who's in charge, doll." He pumps harder, and tears spring in my eyes as my body twitches for air.

He grunts, pushing deeper and stills, cum spurs down my throat, and he releases my nose.

I wheeze for air, and he chuckles softly, brushing the tears from my cheek.

"Fuck, I love you."

He softly pulls me from under the desk, placing me on his lap. I'm still panting as I try to understand what he just said.

His fingers graze over my lips, gliding lower, over my breast and stomach, and then he dips them under my dress. Trailing them over my bare pussy.

"You're dripping on me, doll."

My face heats as lifts me on the desk, the cold wood chills through me. He grabs my knees, roughly parting my legs, and I yelp as my pussy hits the wood.

"Look how pretty." He inches closer, his lips trail over my leg, teasing higher, and I lean back, relaxing my body.

A soft chuckle leaves him as he murmurs. "Let's hope dad doesn't walk in." With a wink, he parts my pussy with his fingers, flicking his tongue over my clit.

I twitch, and he laughs. "Are you a little sore?"

"Y-yes," I stammer.

"Do you remember what I said?"

I vigorously nod, trying to control the smile that I wants to creep onto my lips.

"Say it," he orders, circling my clit with his tongue.

Fuck, he's so close. Torturing me as my hips buck, needing him on me.

"Kiss it better."

He hums. "Good girl." His lips latch around my clit, and he gently sucks, flicking his tongue at the same time, and I scream.

"Fuck!" My hips buck quicker, and my fingers tugs through his hair, needing him closer.

My thighs tighten around his head.

"I'm coming," I scream as my pussy pulses and my core spasms, and I break.

My body trembles as my orgasm crashes through me.

He releases my clit, his tongue gently brushing over it with a hum. His lips and chin glisten from my orgasm.

Fuck, that felt good.

Loud footsteps come closer, and Carter's gaze widens as he releases my legs.

A strong hand grabs my hair and pulls me from the desk.

"Dad," Carter yells.

"You know that I don't want this here. Not in my office!" He yells back.

I claw at his hand, screaming to let me go. "Please."

I should have listened to Carter when he warned me, instead of following this need to test my stepdad, wanting to know his darkest part.

He tosses me in the living room and paces in front of me. His fingers rake through his greying hair as he mumbles something under his breath.

"Daddy," I say as I try to crawl closer.

He sighs, and his pacing stops as he fumbles with his belt. "I didn't tell you. I should have, but still." He swallows thickly as he rolls his belt in his hand until I see what he's doing.

The belt is folded in two, hanging down, and I know this will be my punishment.

The one I wanted, or at least thought I wanted.

"Turn around," he orders.

I shake my head, inching back. "I won't do it again, please."

My eyes find Carter's, his gaze without emotion, and I slowly turn.

"I *was* proud of you, for what you did last night. I should praise you for that, but we have to have some rules in this house," he starts, his words stinging me, and I lay my head on the carpet, the same one I sat on as they shot their cum over me.

"Ass up," he snaps.

I roll my dress higher, baring myself before him, and I hear him inhale sharply.

"Fuck," he curses, grazing the cold leather of his belt over my heated skin. "My office is the only place you're not allowed to be your filthy whore self and so is your mom's room."

"I'm sorry," I cry, but it's in vain.

I hear it first, the leather slicing through the air, and then a silence before I hear it again; this time, it's coming closer.

The leather snaps on my bare ass, and I jolt forward.

My skin burns and stings from the impact.

"Count," my stepfather snaps.

I inch back, "one."

Clenching my eyes shut, I hear it again. My ass trembles, and so do my legs. The leather connects hard, and I scream.

"Count!"

"Two," I quickly yell, my pussy trembles. My chest heaves, my heart races as my body won't stop shaking. Adrenaline coursing through my veins as my ass burns.

It comes again, the harsh sting and burn, but it's softer. It *feels* softer.

"Three," I groan, my hips tilting slightly as my back arches further.

He teases my sore skin with the belt, brushing it over the burn before he kneels behind me. I jerk away as his hand kneads my ass, rubbing circles over my tender skin.

"Rules, angel, we have to have rules."

*Rules you never told me* is what I want to say back, but I keep my lips sealed as I know the warning Carter told me. Knowing this is my own doing.

"I will write them down for you," he muses, his fingers grazing over my pussy.

"Do you want to feel better?" he asks, and my insatiable pussy throbs in need.

"Yes," I breathe.

There is a moment of silence, and I hesitantly glance back, watching Carter and my stepdad exchange glances.

My stepdad moves in front of me, his finger hooks under my chin as he tilts my face. There is no anger in his eyes as he gazes down at me. A soft smile tugs on his lips.

"Ride me again, angel," he says and strips before lying on the carpet. "Take what you want, just like I do to you."

There is the balance again.

But what surprises me even more are my own feelings and thoughts.

Why don't I hate this? Why aren't I furious about what he did? And how is it even possible that the only word that tickles my tongue is—more.

# Chapter Twenty-Three

More.

A simple word, but one that is driving me insane.

As I crawl over his naked body, my fingers tease over his chest, remembering how good it felt when my hand wrapped around his throat.

I lower myself, letting his cock glide inside me as a gasp leaves my lips. My walls stretch, wrapping around his thick cock, and I shiver.

He pushes me back slightly, pressing on my stomach, and I whimper, feeling the head nudge against that sweet spot inside me.

I roll my hips, and moans spill from my lips as his eyes burn into mine. Carter watches us, pealing the clothes from his body, and my core clenches in response.

"Eyes on me," Daddy orders, and I do. Not daring to defy him, even though I feel that slight tingle in my clit begging me to.

My pace quickens, and a hand pushes me forward. My fingers trail up, curling around Daddy's throat as I feel Carter behind me.

Daddy takes over, slowly thrusting as I feel something cold drip on my ass.

I whimper, trying to move, but I'm kept in place.

"Fight all you want," Carter chuckles. "but this." His finger dips inside my ass, stretching it as I feel the tip of his cock nudged under it. "Is mine to take."

Moans fall, and I tilt my hip slightly as he pushes his cock in.

"Fuck," I whimper, burring my face in the crook of Daddy's neck.

Carter doesn't stop; he thrusts through with a groan, and they move in sync.

"It's too much," I cry. The tension doesn't fade; my body clenches, tightening as they move faster.

Carter grips my hips, and I shake my head, tears rolling down my cheeks.

"Spank her," Daddy orders.

Carter doesn't wait, and a harsh slap follows. I cry out, my back curves as my ass heats. His hand trails up my spine, his fingers intertwine with my hair, and he tilts my head up.

My sight is blurred, and I blink away the tears to see Brad standing in the distance. His jaw ticks, and my eyes fall to the bulge in his pants.

"You don't want to disappoint your stepbrother, right?" Carter taunts.

My heart aches, and with a trembling hand, I reach for Brad. He smiles softly, tossing the clothes off his body and rubs his cock.

As Brad's cock glides over my lips, as Daddy's hand teases my clit, as they pump inside me, my insides coil, building up and balancing on a thin edge.

Brad slides his cock inside my mouth. "You want to come, little slut? You want to come over your Daddy's and brother's cock?"

I shiver at his words; my pussy tightens, and my stepdad groans beneath me.

"Do you like being filled by all three of us?" Brad teases.

I moan around his cock, the vibration making him moan.

"Do you want us to destroy you?"

I swallow, inching back, even though I can't move.

He grins at me; Carter slams harshly as Daddy plunges deeper.

"It doesn't matter, we will."

I know what I signed up for; I know I shouldn't let panic and fear rise. I said yes; I took the step when Daddy came home.

Maybe if I said no, he would have let me walk. I hold onto that thought, seeing this all as my choice.

I love who I have become, who they let me become.

I feel wanted, desired, and loved.

What more can I want?

Brad grabs my head, fucking my mouth at the same pace as his brother. I gag, choke, and cry. My body is being used like a doll, a slut, and a whore.

And then I hear it, the soft whisper against my ear.

The balance I crave most.

"Come, angel."

The wall I built crashes, and my orgasm rakes through me like a tidal wave, squirting all over the cocks inside me.

Carter stills, his cum filling my ass as I ride through. The salty taste comes next as Brad pushes his cock down my throat, painting it with his cum.

My stepbrothers leave me, and before I can get my baring, Daddy tosses me over; he grabs my ankles, pushing them to my face as he slams with all his might.

I scream under him as he destroys me. I claw at his hands, but Brad quickly grabs them, keeping them above my head.

Daddy groans, fucking me like the beast he is.

Not a sound can leave me as I take all he gives. My pussy quivers around his cock, and I don't know if I can hold back my orgasm.

Pulling my bottom lip behind my teeth, I fight it, pushing it back, but I can't, not as he grips my ass cheeks hard, pounding into me.

But I made it.

I gasp for air as he stills, his cum filling me, and he slowly pulls out.

I'm panting, my body shaking as he releases my ankles and parts my legs, wanting my destroyed pussy on display.

"Look how pretty," he sighs and leans down, dipping his tongue in me.

"You don't think he wouldn't let you come?" Brad taunts.

Soft moans leave me as Daddy thrusts his tongue, his finger plunges into my ass, and I squirm. His other hand moves up, toying with my clit, and my hips buck.

My back arches, and my eyes roll back as pleasure consumes me.

A sharp tug on my nipple makes my eyes flutter open; Carter's lips latch around my perked nipple, sucking and softly nibbling it.

"Oh, god," I moan as it all feels too much. "Please, please, can I come?" My eyes snap to Brad, waiting for him to say yes.

He grins at me as he crawls down; without releasing my wrists, he flicks his tongue over my other nipple.

My body jerks, my insides clench, and I'm a whimpering mess. Waiting to hear that word, I need to let everything go.

It's all too consuming, my clit, my pussy, my ass, my nipples...

I hear a muffled groan coming from Daddy, the order I craved.

"Come."

I let it all go, stop keeping my trembling core under control, and spill all I have, covering Daddy's face.

He hums and flicks his tongue one last time over my clit.

"We taste divine, you and me," he says as his dark blue eyes lock with mine.

His words hit me hard, and a tear falls.

Carter is by my side, curling his arms around me. "You did so good."

I bury my head in his chest, not wanting them to see how they broke me.

"Come let's get her cleaned up," my stepfather says, and Carter lifts me up.

I don't open my eyes as I savor this moment. All their hands on my body, gentle and caring as praises fall from their lips.

"Look at me," Brad orders, and my eyes slowly flutter open. "You have no idea how much control you have."

Me? Control?

My brows pinch as I softy laugh.

He grabs my chin, forcing me to look at him. "You can make this all stop."

"That's not true."

I don't want it to stop anymore, but I never had a choice in the beginning.

"It is."

"Then why did you never stop when I asked?"

"Because you didn't want me to stop. You were lying to us and yourself."

"But not anymore," Carter adds.

My eyes find Daddy's, and he smiles at me. "I never took anything from you." He tilts his head, showing the bruises on his throat, and my face heats.

"I only gave what you wanted."

What I wanted...

My lips part as I try to say he's wrong, try to speak up and tell him I was tricked into all this, but it doesn't come.

Because it's not true, not anymore.

I wish I could say what they are doing is wrong, and maybe it is, seeing they are my stepbrothers and stepdad, but I wouldn't want to change it.

I can pretend they made me think like that, that they twisted my mind in such a way that I changed into this needy person. Needy for their attention and touch.

But I think they only showed me what I had inside me all this time.

"And what do I want next?" I ask, not knowing the answer myself.

I'm leaving for college in a few days; everyone will go back to their lives as if this summer never happened.

"Whatever you want."

# CHAPTER TWENTY-FOUR

He wasn't joking, as my eyes are fixed on the piece of paper on my desk in my room. He made what seems like a simple list but isn't.

Some of the rules I recognize. The 'no panties' rule, the 'wear a dress for easy access.' All courtesy of Carter.

Rule number 7. Courtesy of Dad.

I thought I would feel stuck and that I would hate this list with everything I got. But I don't. It feels safe somehow.

Rules

    1. Your sex, ass, and mouth are ours at any time.

    2. You will let us fuck you in public places.

    3. You will not wear any undergarments.

4. You will only wear dresses in our presence; we want easy access at all times.

5. You will let us share you, but you belong to us. No one else is allowed to touch you.

6. You will play our games, and even if you fight, you will lose.

7. You may sleep with who you want, fuck us in our sleep as we will do you.

8. You will not touch yourself without permission.

9. You will not come without permission.

10. You will earn your orgasms by being good, and you will get punished when you're not.

11. You're not allowed to please us or take pleasure from us in the office or your mother's room.

12. You will trust that we know what is best for you.

Rule 12—Trust. I swallow hard, knowing trusting Brad again will be difficult. Even though ever since Daddy got home, he went back to his quiet self; I'm not over what kind of mind games he played on me.

I can't tell when he speaks the truth or is toying with me. I want to trust him; I want to believe he cares, but it needs time, I guess.

Today is the last day, though.

Daddy has locked himself in his office, and I let him be as I see the suitcase by the front door.

Carter's suitcase.

My heart aches, as I wish we had more time together. But I can't expect him to give up his job in London, just like he can't ask me to move with him and drop out of college.

"Carter," I call out as I walk through the living room.

He hums, and I find him at the kitchen counter.

"You're leaving?"

His gaze snaps to mine, and he slowly nods. "Summer is over." He smiles, but he can't hide the hurt in his eyes, the one that makes me feel relieved.

I'm not the only one.

"I don't want you to go," I say.

He sighs and pats the stool beside him. "Me either."

I sit beside him, not knowing what to say next, as he takes my hand. "Do you want to go out tonight?"

The last time I went out with one of my stepbrothers, I got fucked in an alleyway without me knowing it was Brad.

A blush rises on my cheek. "I would like that."

## Carter

I hate this; I hate that I have to go back. It almost felt like the first time when Dad ordered me to go because he feared I would do something to Katie.

I didn't, though, well. I eventually did. A dark chuckle rumbles in my chest as I walk behind the waiter who brings me and Katie to our table.

She looks stunning in a tight black dress, and I'm sure if I lean back, I can see she isn't wearing anything underneath.

Good fucking girl.

My hand rests on her lower back, guiding her to her seat. As I take mine, she speaks up.

"No, I want you to sit next to me," she says quickly.

My brows knit as the waiter looks at us weirdly. This isn't the kind of place where we can sit nudged together, but if she wants it, who am I to say no?

I grab my seat and drag it next to hers. She smiles and moves slightly to give me more room.

"Better," she breathes, and I take her hand.

This need to touch her at any second is killing me, but it seems she has the same feelings.

Our intimate seating doesn't go unnoticed, some here know she's my little stepsister as we didn't go to another town for dinner.

But it seems Katie doesn't care one bit. It astonishes me how strong she has become in the last few weeks.

The weak little girl has been replaced by a strong woman, one I want to have by my side for the rest of my life.

My lips tug in a smile as she gushes about college, and my hand dips under the table. And I place my napkin on top, shielding my touch from prying eyes as I brush over her bare leg.

Her words get caught in her throat, and she stares at me with wide eyes.

"You were saying," I say, teasing my fingers over her inner thigh.

She stammers slightly, her gaze shifting around the restaurant. "I-I said I was looking forward to seeing my friends again."

I hum, my fingers grazing higher, teasing her wet pussy. "It seems you're looking forward to something else." My voice is a low whisper, and she slowly parts her legs, just enough for me to tease further.

The waiter comes to bring our main course, and Katie tries to close her legs. I grin, plunging my finger inside her, and she gasps, gripping the table.

"Carter," she whispers sternly, and I lean closer.

"Remember the rules, doll."

Her eyes narrow, and I slowly, very slowly, thrust my fingers back and forth. My voice is low, making sure no one overhears my next words. "Now, relax your legs and let me make you come."

Her thighs shake against my hand, and she slowly parts them again. "Good girl."

As the waiter leaves us, I pick up my pace, pumping my fingers as I press my thumb on her clit. She pulls her lips behind her teeth and clenches her eyes shut as she tries to keep still.

Her hips buck slightly, her breathing shallows, and her lips pull free. A soft moan vibrates from them, and I say what pushes her over the edge.

"Come for me, doll."

She bucks once more, and then squirts, coating my hand.

"Good girl," I whisper, and her eyes snap to mine.

There it is, that look in her eyes telling me she will do anything just to make me proud. I inch closer, softly pressing my lips on hers as I pull my fingers from her tight cunt.

I didn't lie when I told her I love her; I truly didn't.

She leans into my kiss, his fingers rake through my hair, and she tugs me closer. I groan as our tongues stroke each other.

I pull back, leaning my forehead against hers.

"I'm yours, Katie," I say, meaning every word.

"You aren't just saying that?" She edges back, her eyes fixed on mine.

I shake my head. "I won't play with your heart, I promise."

I was furious with Brad and even my dad for patting his shoulder, saying he did good. We all have our dark desires, and even though I will take what I want from Katie, I will never play with her heart.

She clears her throat, peeling herself away from me. "I'm going to clean up."

I nod, leaning back as I watch her hurry to the bathroom. The insides of her thighs glistening with her own cum, makes me grin.

She can fight me, she can fight my touch, she can fight the feelings she has for me. But we know I will win.

Always.

# CHAPTER TWENTY-FIVE

*Brad*

She left me, left with my brother. Only this time, I couldn't tag along.

It wouldn't matter; I won't let her out of my sight, even when she goes back to Harvard. I will be there, in every corner, in every room.

I don't know what to do as something is nagging inside me. I'm not jealous; I enjoy watching her being taken, knowing she will get my cum too.

I crave how it feels when she's a crying mess between all of us.

And it still feels like it isn't enough.

As if I'm missing something.

Perhaps I am.

And I know we all should have our moments with our play thing alone, but I somehow can't.

Not now.

Not after I've seen her come all over my brother's fingers, leaving me painfully hard.

But I know the cure for that.

As I stalk behind Katie going into the bathroom, I know she goes in to clean herself up, but there is no need for that. Not while I'm here.

There she is, drying the inside of her legs with a paper towel, not even noticing I'm here.

I wear the same outfit as our moment in the alleyway, my hoody hiding my face, and the smell of cinnamon wafts off me.

There it is. She freezes, and I hear her sniff the air. I move behind her, not making a sound, and as she straightens herself, she sees me through the mirror.

She doesn't move as I edge closer. "I don't like it when you leave me." My words are honest, not daring to play with this.

She shakes her head. "Don't do that."

Tilting my head to the side, my hands curl around her waist, pulling her ass against my cock. "Do what?"

"Don't pretend you care about anything other than fucking me."

I blink, the pieces falling together. Shit. It isn't that she has control over me; it is because I let her have it. I care—I started to care for her even though I never wanted that.

"Maybe I want it all." My hand grazes over the hem of her dress, sliding it up over her ass.

She whimpers, her eyes fixed on her pussy as I rub her clit.

"You like this, seeing yourself get fucked through the mirror?"

She slowly nods, and I free my cock with my other hand. Pushing her legs apart with my knee, I line the head of my cock against her entrance and glide inside her.

I push in as deep as possible, and still, savoring how her cunt wraps around my dick, squeezing with every stroke her clit gets from my fingers.

"You feel so good, little slut," I groan, pulling out before I thrust in again.

She arches her back, moving with me. Our moans fill the room, echoing off the tilted wall.

A harsh knock makes me stop. "Katie, are you okay?"

I smile as I hear Carter's voice.

"She's all good, brother," I shout back, pumping in her again.

He quickly gets inside and locks the door behind him.

A grin spreads on his face as he sees our plaything, her skin flushed from pleasure, her lips parted, and soft moans spill.

"You like his cock inside you," He taunts, and her pussy spasms in response.

"Yes," she moans.

I slam harder; her stomach nudged against the sink.

"Do you want us both, or do I have to *make* you?"

Her lips curve slightly.

Oh, our dirty little slut.

"Make me," she says.

And I still, afraid I'll come just by hearing her say that.

"What do you think, brother, can her tight cunt take us both?"

She blinks, her lips tremble.

I reach down, curling my fingers beside my cock, stretching slightly.

"It's a tight fit, but I'm sure my doll won't disappoint us."

She squirms in my grip, a small hint of panic surges in her gaze, and I turn us to Carter, leisurely pumping inside her as his fingers replace mine, stretching her as best as he can.

She claws at his chest, trying to push him away. Her legs close, tightening around his wrist, and I grab them, yanking them apart, and slam inside her as punishment.

"Fight harder if you want him to stop," I whisper, but he will never stop.

Neither will I.

She cries, and Carter quickly covers her mouth with his other hand. Not wanting to get disturbed by worried staff.

He hisses as she bites him, but he doesn't pull away; he pushes his hand deeper inside her mouth and pussy in a warning, and she stills.

"Good girl," he praises, lining his cock beside mine. I inch out, giving some room as he thrusts inside, and then I edge deeper beside him as I hear her muffled screams.

We're slow and cautious, waiting for the pain and tension to fade from her body. Her whimpers change, her body relaxes, and we pick up our pace.

She softly moans against Carter's hand and leans back, resting her head on my chest, letting pleasure take over.

His grip on her thigh weakens, and I snake between her and Carter, trailing to her clit as I want to feel her come around us.

Gently, I rub circle's over her clit, and she tilts her head to mine. Carter releases her mouth, and I don't wait as I claim her lips with mine.

She tastes heavenly as my tongue strokes hers. Our moans vibrate around them.

Her hand snakes around my neck, pulling me closer, and my cock twitches, on the verge of coming.

"Not yet, little brother," Carter teases, and I peek at him through my lashes as he tilts closer, his lips brushing over her throat. She shivers at his touch, her cunt milking me in the process, showing how close she is as well.

I grin against her lips and mumble. "Come with me."

She moans, and my fingers work faster, bringing us to our climax.

Carter curses as he feels it, too; there is no going back as she squeezes tightly around us. I slam one last time, pushing us all over the edge as Carter and my cock twitch inside her, our cum spurting out.

My lips break from hers, and she twitches against me as her juices come next, coating our cocks.

"Fuck," she breathes. "I'm going to miss you two."

"It's just a few months and then we see each other at Christmas break," Carter says.

Her eyes light up as they shift between mine and my brother's.

"All of us?"

I chuckle. "It will be a little harder though. Your mother will probably be home, so we have to be careful."

Her eyes widen slightly, just for a brief moment, before her lips curve. "Or even more fun."

Oh, little slut, it sure will.

# CHAPTER TWENTY-SIX

*Katie*

I'm sore, in a good way, because this time I wanted it. And yet, my heart aches as I pack my bag to head back to college. Carter left after our dinner last night, well, our half dinner. I chuckle; my face heats as I remember what we did at our table and what happened in the ladies' room.

God, how can I survive without them?

My hand trembles as tears spring in my eyes. I know I have to leave, get back to my life, and leave this fantasy behind.

A soft knock on the door makes me blink, quickly wiping away the tears that roll over my cheek. I watch as the door opens, and my stepdad walks in.

"Are you okay, angel?"

I sniff and shake my head. Not knowing what to say because we all know I can't lie. I can't pretend.

"What do you want?" he asks as he stalks closer.

"I want to feel better," I whisper, staring at my half-packed bag.

He bends down, hooking his fingers under my chin, and tilts my head, forcing me to meet his gaze.

"I can make you feel better." He grins, and that small tingle emerges.

I shift on my knees as I hold his gaze. "How?"

"I can make sure you won't forget about us." He rubs his thumb over my lips as his other hand unbuckles his belt.

How can I ever?

"Isn't mom getting home any second?" I rub my thighs together; the idea of getting caught awakens something in me.

"Then we shouldn't waste any time." He pulls out his cock, softly stroking it as my eyes fix on the head. A small droplet of pre-cum leaks from the tip, and I inch closer.

Softly, I lick the head, swirling my tongue over the pre-cum. His hand brushes over my cheek, moving to the back of my head as he pushes me on further with a grunt.

The sound rakes through my spine, and my pussy clenches around nothing.

I don't know if he heard us or if he has a sixth sense for these kinds of things, but I hear him cautiously coming closer.

"Doesn't she look pretty, sucking Daddy's cock," my stepdad muses at Brad.

Brad chuckles darkly and edges closer. "She sure does."

He moves behind me, tugging my dress up, and lets his hands wander over my bare skin. "Do you want us both, little slut?"

My legs tremble as his hand dips between them, and I hum around Daddy's cock, tilting my hips back in need of more.

Daddy's cock plunges deeper as Brad's fingers thrust inside me.

"Soaking wet," he whispers. "Always ready for me, aren't you, little slut."

My walls clench around his fingers, pulling him in further, and he shifts behind me. I hear his zipper opening and feel his cock slide through my cheeks, nudging against my entrance.

I moan around Daddy's cock, and he fucks me harder, gripping my hair tightly as he chases his release.

"Fuck, I'm going to miss you," he says, forcing me to take him deeper.

I grip his hips, keeping myself steady as Brad glides inside me. My pussy quivers, still sore from yesterday. And yet, it feels so good.

His pace is slow, and his hand snakes around my waist, moving to my aching clit. I whimper as he rubs his fingers over it; my hip buck and my stomach coils.

A phone rings in the distance, and Daddy curses under his breath.

"Looks like he has to go," Brad whispers in my ear, soft enough so no one else hears it.

I suck harder, wanting all Daddy can give me as he pushes his cock down my throat. I swallow, my throat working around his shaft, and cum spurts down. My eyes close, savoring the feel as he brushes his finger over my cheek.

"My perfect whore," he praises and softly pulls out. He kneels before me, cupping my face with his hands. "You're ours, remember that."

"I know, Daddy," I breathe as Brad keeps his pace slow.

"Such a good girl." He tilts closer, gently pressing his lips on mine. I freeze, and so does Brad. But as Daddy teases my lips with his tongue, my lips part, welcoming him.

He groans as our tongues move around each other, and as the phone rings again, he pulls back with a sigh. "I'm sorry, angel. I got to pick up your mother." He smiles and gives me one last peck before he leaves without a second glance.

I gulp as Brad's arm tugs me closer. "It seems it is just you and me now."

I shiver, and he moves again, thrusting harder with every second. Toying with my clit as his other arm keeps me in place.

As if he fears, I might move away, but I won't.

I move with him, and my pussy wraps around his cock tighter as my orgasm builds quickly.

His grip loosens, his hand moves to my back, and he harshly pushes me down on the floor, my ass curves up on its own, and he rails in me, his finger digging into my skin as he holds my hips tight.

"Say you're mine," he grunts.

I stammer with the words as all the sounds I make are moans and cries.

"Say it!" He slaps my ass, his pace not faltering.

"Fuck, yes, I'm yours!" I cry out.

He groans, his upper body leaning over mine as his thrusts slow slightly. "Come with me then."

He chuckles as my pussy vibrates around his pumping cock, my hips spasm. Sweat trickles down my body as I stop holding back, stop controlling what has been trying to escape.

My core tightens almost painfully, and I squirt over Brad's cock.

"My good, *good* little slut." He leans back, glancing at his cock before he stills, spurting his cum inside me.

I go limp on the floor, panting, as my body shakes.

He gently pulls out and lies next to me, brushing his fingers over my spine as he stares into my eyes.

"Are you going to miss me too?"

The corner of my lip twitches as I want to smile.

"Yes," I breathe, relieved that the piece he broke is slowly healing, and I feel like I can trust him again.

I know it was his game, his trick, the thing he craves.

But maybe, as he gazes at me now, maybe he regrets it.

Just a little bit.

The pain I felt earlier, the sadness that moved through me, has faded as I head downstairs with my bag. Ready to go back to my life. My normal life.

Brad is with me at every step as if he doesn't want to miss a second. I don't get him, not truly. Maybe I never did.

My brows knit as I see another bag by the door.

"What is that?" I ask as I point at it.

"Oh, that's mine," Brad says as he zips up his jacket.

"Where are you going?" I thought he would stay here, seeing he lives here.

"Wherever you're going." He says it so simply as if it means nothing. But it means so much. Too much.

My heart races as I stammer with my next words.

"Katie?" He grabs my shoulder and moves in front of my stare. "Look at me."

I blink. "Why are you coming with me?" I stare into his eyes; his jaw ticks, and he looks hurt... Is that even possible?

"You don't want me?"

I shake my head. "I do, but I didn't think you would come with me to college. What are you going to do there?"

"Be with you." He shrugs and takes my bag. "It's pretty simple, really."

"Really?"

He grabs his bag next and walks out the front door to his pick-up. "It couldn't be simpler."

"What?" I run after him as I try to get what he's saying. Did Carter and Daddy put him up to this? Do they want to keep an eye on me? Making sure I won't let anyone else touch me?

He tosses the bags in the backseat and opens the door for me. "You like me?"

My brows knit. Do I like him? As much as I can without getting hurt. I have to protect myself and my heart. "I think so."

"And I like fucking you. And Christmas takes too long, so this is the solution."

He likes fucking me? I sigh, taking it. "Only the fucking part?"

He scratches the back of his head. "And you're nice to talk to."

Yeah, because we talk so much. I pinch the bridge of my nose; a soft chuckle leaves me. "It's okay if you like me, see me as more than just a fuck toy."

What am I doing? Do I want him to say that he cares? Do I even want him to care? God, why is he so confusing?

"Maybe," he pauses and glances at his watch. "We should go before dad and your mom get back."

The corner of my lip curves, having a feeling he's doing something he shouldn't. "Don't you want to say good-bye?"

"No, I'm good."

"He doesn't know?" I taunt, stepping closer.

"He will know once he gets home." He nods, more to himself than me, as if he's trying to convince himself one last time that he's doing the right thing.

"And Carter?"

"He will know once dad finds out," he pauses, "probably."

"Are you sure you want to do this?"

"I go where you go, Katie."

I laugh and shake my head as I climb into the passenger seat. A soft breeze tickles my thighs, and I hear Brad groan behind me.

"Panties?"

"I thought I was leaving, alone. So yes."

He grins. "You know the rules."

A blush reddens my cheeks, and he closes the door and hurries to the other side. I don't know what will happen next, what will become of us, because I never saw this coming.

But then again, I never knew my summer would be this intense.

I can't really use another word for it or tell anyone what happened. So, if someone asks, I'll say it was an intense summer, and I wish it would have lasted longer.

I don't know what the future brings, but now, as Brad's pick-up roars to life and we take off, I can't wait to find out.

# CHAPTER TWENTY-SEVEN

## *A few months later*

Here we go, almost back home after I spent the last few months at my dorm with my... well... I have no clue what Brad and I are to each other, but the last months were interesting.

Brad kept his word and turned into my shadow. Everywhere I went, he went. He even managed to sneak into some of my classes.

I want to say that I found it annoying or a bit too much.

But I loved every second of it. No one knew he was my stepbrother, and it almost seemed as if we were a normal couple. *Almost.*

His *devotion* to me, since that's what I'm choosing to call him haunting me with every step I take, has become more. I don't hesitate at the thought that he actually cares for me. I care about him, I know that. I can't give him up even though I should know better.

I wished I could keep him away or my growing feelings, but there is no denying it anymore.

*I crave him.* I ache for his touch, his words, his low voice in my ear as he defiles me.

But he cares for me too, even though he tries hard to hide it.

Maybe that's why he likes to *take* me, to degrade me—wanting to be in complete control, me at his mercy.

If he didn't have feelings for me, he wouldn't glower at every man who approaches me, wouldn't have spent so much time with me, and wouldn't reliably be there. Not to mention the way he looks at me. A way he thinks I don't notice.

I might never know what goes on in his head, why he wants me, and he can continue to pretend he doesn't care. And I'll pretend I don't know he does.

I shift in my seat as he drives us up the driveway. A smile curves as I see we are the first ones here. The grin won't falter as he grabs our bags from the back seat and steps out. Heading to where it all began. I move quickly, jumping out of his truck and following behind him.

There is no caution in his stride as he opens the door and goes inside, tossing the bags at the stairs as I shut the door behind us.

Silence lays thick around as he turns to me and crawls closer, like the predator he is. His dark eyes rake over my body and that teasing smile lets me know what he's thinking.

The heat of his body seeps into mine. "Alone again, little slut." The words move through me, pooling between my legs.

"Yes, we are," I say, inching closer until my body is flush against his.

He groans softly, his fingers digging into my hips. "That's how you want it?"

"I don't know what you mean," I taunt.

He chuckles darkly and lifts me in a blink. I squeal as he tosses me over his shoulder, my dress sliding up, and he palms my ass as he walks into the living room.

"Brad, we can't." My words have no meaning; I know anyone can walk through that door at any moment, and I don't care. Not as my body aches for him.

He chuckles, his fingers dip between my legs. "You don't want me?"

There it is, that tiny pang of guilt he pushes on me as he makes *himself* believe I wouldn't want *him*. All of him.

He doesn't wait for an answer as he thrusts two fingers in me, and my pussy clenches.

"It feels like you do," he muses as a soft moan spills from my lips.

His touch leaves as he flings me on the couch. My eyes lock onto his as he peels the clothes from his body, tossing them to the ground until my dress is the only thing standing in our way.

He moves torturously slow, pushing the boundaries, wanting to get caught. His fingers hook under my dress, and he strips it from my heated skin. His gaze darkens, lust filling every feature as his eyes focus on my aching pussy, all ready for what he's planning.

He stares at me for a moment, and I unhook my bra, casting it to the side.

My nipples perk as his stare burns me while mine trails over his body. His strong shoulders and chest, his sculpted abs, but there is one thing I like the most.

He edges closer, his fingers graze over my cheek and then rake through my hair. With a gentle tug, he tilts my head back as he crawls over me. His cock is right there waiting for me, and I wet my lips as I can almost taste him.

"I'm going to make your pussy jealous of your mouth." I don't get a word out as he slams into my throat, grunting while I choke around his cock.

"I'm all that matters, little slut," he snarls, picking up his pace, tears prickle my eyes, and I struggle for my next breath, clawing at his thighs.

I have no control over how he's using me, and I know I'm sick for loving every part of this and needing this even more than he does.

Wanting everything.

My core begs, tightening almost painfully as I squirm beneath him. He pushes inside me once more, stilling as I swallow, working my throat muscles around him as he trembles.

This part, this moment, makes me feel powerful, that even though he uses me for his pleasure, it's only me that can give him that. A whine leaves me as he pulls out. I wanted to taste him, to drown in his cum as it slipped down my throat and over my lips, but I know he has other plans.

He takes my hand as he sits, pulling me over him as he says, "Get over here."

I move, crawling over his body as we stare at each other.

"You're going to sit on my cock and ride me." He grabs my hips, jerking me down on him and filling me in one go.

"Fuck," I cry out, my walls stretching full as his cock stills inside me.

"Ride me," he orders sharply. I roll my hips, and he slaps my ass harshly. "Now!"

I gasp and obey, a soft smile tugging on my lips as my pace quickens, taking him deep as I move my hips.

His jaw clenches, and he grabs my ass, his fingers digging into my skin.

It's *too* soft. *Too soft for him.*

Another point in the 'he likes me' column.

Neither of us notices we aren't alone anymore until my head is yanked back, and his brother hisses in my face. "You like that?"

He pushes me further down, and I whimper softly. "You like riding your brother like a dirty little slut?"

My cheeks redden, and I moan in response, unable to answer as fear prickles my scalp with the stormy stare that shifts between him and Brad.

"Fuck I missed you," Carter says and pushes me sharply forward, spreading my ass and freeing his cock, not even taking the time to take off his clothes.

As I turn my head to take a peek, Brad captures my lips with his, forcing me to stay with him as Carter prepares me. Brad has taken over, tilting his hip, almost the same slow move as his tongue against mine.

"I missed you, so *so* much," Carter says more to himself than me as he guides the tip of his cock inside me.

My whimpers are muffled as Brad doesn't let me go. His arms wrap around me, keeping me tightly against him, leaving me unable to move, even an inch.

Carter thrusts further, and my body quivers between them, trying to contain the orgasm that's about to burst.

They move in sync, every thrust harder than the one before, and I need to breathe. I need to scream.

I bite down on Brad's lip, and he groans. The taste of copper tickles my tongue as I tilt my head back, taking a deep breath.

"Fuck," he grunts with a grin, a single droplet of blood painted on his lip. "Bite me again and see what happens." The warning coils through me as I don't see anger in his eyes but mischief, daring me to do it again so he can punish me for it.

Carter grabs my hair and jerks it back. "I heard you kept her all to yourself." He stares at Brad, narrowing his eyes as he leans over me. Brad laughs, changing his thrusting pace. "And it was the best months ever, brother."

My pussy clenches around Brad's pumping cock as I can't hold it back anymore. As he feels my restraint breaking, his eyes snap at mine. "Come."

I moan in relief, letting it all go as my body spasms between them, taking them over the edge with me as my grip on their cocks tightens.

"Good girl," Carter says gently in my ear.

Brad softly strokes my bottom lip, and I sigh, sweaty, dripping, exhausted as I rest my head on his chest.

A car door closes loudly, and I curse under my breath. Carter jumps off me, making me winch as his cock leaves me, and I scamper off Brad, catching my dress as Carter tosses it and follows after him with Brad close behind me.

The front door creaks open as we run up the stairs, cum dripping down my thighs as I giggle softly, earning a slap from Brad to silence me.

The upstairs carpet floors muffle my steps as I run into my room and to the bathroom, quickly getting a shower, even though I don't want to wash them off my skin, having this need to show Daddy what we've been doing. Just to test where we are.

He never reached out, nothing, and it's making me anxious. Carter, on the other hand, texted me daily to check up on me, assuring me that what happened during the summer break wasn't just a moment but so much more to him.

But what exactly, he wouldn't say.

After cleaning up enough that I don't have cum running down my thighs and changing into some clean clothes, I head back downstairs to greet my mom and stepdad as if I didn't get fucked by my stepbrothers a few seconds ago.

"Hi, sweetie," my mom says as she hugs me tightly at the bottom of the stairs.

# CHAPTER TWENTY-EIGHT

M y mother and I have a simple relationship; it has always been like that, and I don't see it changing soon. She's a kind and warm person, but there was always something missing in our relationship.

Her own plans were her top priority; nothing could keep her away from chasing her goals. Even though I never figured them out, she was just not *really* present. And that's okay, I guess. I turned out just fine.

Well, *fine* isn't the right word, perhaps, but I'm happy, and she's happy, and that's what's important.

And now as I sit at the dining table, I don't know how to act around my stepdad. Not when I realize there's a possibility he doesn't want me anymore.

He smiles, maybe even noticing my discomfort and asks, "How was campus, angel?"

Just that word on his tongue reminds me of every time he's been inside me, and I flush. "It's good. School is going well, but it's nice to be back."

His smile changes as this glint roams through his eyes. I gulp, and my thighs clench together.

"It's nice to have you back," he says.

The conversation is shockingly normal compared to the tense air around me. The weight of my stepbrothers' eyes, the heat of my stepdad's gaze, and my mom is oblivious to it all.

Does she know? Does she have any idea that I've been used, bent over, fucked by each man at this table separately, together, in plenty of ways and situations that no sane person would allow?

My thoughts bounce and heat my core until I'm a squirming mess.

Then, when I see my mom smile at my stepdad, her gaze so loving and pure, I swallow the rising lump in the back of my throat. I don't want to think of them being together.

I don't want to think of him talking to her the way he talks to me, fucking her the way he fucks me. If that makes me greedy, so be it. I want to be the only person he wants.

But that's not my choice. It was my choice to let my stepdad fuck me, use me, make me his toy, but I don't want to admit that he's my mom's.

I thought I had all my mess sorted, but now I wonder what will become of all this.

Taking another bite of my food, I stretch my legs out to tease my stepbrothers. Popping my fluffy slippers off, I slide my bare feet higher on Carter's legs, teasing his calves and thighs through his pants.

He cuts me a warning look, and I move my foot to Brad as I try to pay attention to my mom's words. A smile creeps on my lips as Brad shifts in his seat and parts his legs, luring me closer.

His cock grows under my feet, and I do the same to Carter with my other foot. Rubbing over his covered dick until I feel it hardening and then slide to his thigh again.

He nearly chokes on his food when I squeeze his thigh with my toes. Brad's lips are set in a grin, enjoying my tricks.

They know I'm teasing both of them now, and I can hardly hide how much fun it is.

*Do something*, I dare silently. *Retaliate*.

Mom is sitting right there. She could notice any second. And that thought stirs something inside me, pushing me to do more.

"What do you think, Carter?" she asks about the food as she nods to his almost empty plate.

"Perfect, as always," he grits out, as I rub over his cock.

She gently pats his back. "I'm glad."

My stepdad shoots me a look as if he realizes what's going on under the table, one that promises punishment.

But what's he going to do with my mom right there?

"It's so nice to have my whole family at the table," my mom says, looking us over.

Some kind of guilt weighs in my belly, knowing what I'm doing would hurt her, and I peel my touch away from my stepbrothers.

"Very nice," Carter grunts before giving me another sizzling look.

"I've missed this," my stepdad says, his eyes on me. "Having everyone here, happy, healthy, in one place."

"It's great to be back," I agree. "And with Christmas coming up too. I can't wait to shop for everyone and make sure I get the perfect present."

Brad chuckles softly. "I'm sure that'll be easy for you."

My mom's brows pinch. "Well, has everyone had enough?"

"Yes," Carter and Brad say sharply, their gazes burning me.

I know they're talking to me and not her, but she clears the table anyway. "You guys go have a guy's night. I want some time with Katie."

I almost groan. I want to be left alone in my room to see who comes knocking or barging in first. Instead, I get up, grab some plates and head to the kitchen. Disappointment roams inside me as I load in the dishwasher. I know I should have some restraint, but I haven't seen Carter since the summer, and we only have two weeks here.

Closing the dishwasher, my mom grabs a glass of wine. "Come, let's hang up the garlands by the stairs."

It isn't a question; it's a command for me to do the decorations, like every year and then I have to hear about what I did wrong. But does she ever help? No, because why would she?

She asks me about school, and I answer, behaving like she expects.

"So, classes are going well, how about the rest of college?" Mom asks as I work on winding the garland around the banister of the stairs.

"What do you mean?" I ask as the thick garland slides between my fingers.

"I mean, are you dating? You're becoming an adult, baby," she croons. "You can't tell me that a boy hasn't caught your eyes. Maybe even a boyfriend?"

I stammer as I blush. My moves slow as I try to come up with something.

"Just give your dad a heads up. I'm sure he'll have plenty of questions for the poor boy. And prepare the boy for your brothers." She laughs and takes another sip.

"Stepdad and stepbrothers," I correct softly.

She doesn't hear me as my blush intensifies. My eyes find Brad and Carter. Neither seem pleased with the reminder.

We can't really be together.

I know that.

They can't claim me as their girlfriend. They can't let on that they fuck me at all, let alone like me. They can't claim me as anything but their stepsister.

After more decorating and dodging my mom's invasive questions, I head to bed. My mom is stirring the pot, and she doesn't even know it.

She doesn't get that if I started seeing someone else, I'm pretty sure Brad would deck the guy, and Carter would threaten him. I don't even want to think about what my stepdad would do.

Still, those thoughts swirl in my head as I try to get ready to sleep.

# CHAPTER TWENTY-NINE

## *Henry*

She's going to be the death of me, taunting us like that in front of her mother. I shake my head as a smile creeps onto my lips.

I hoped when I saw her again, I would see how wrong I was. Wrong for wanting her, touching her, and making her beg for more.

I tried not to be furious at Brad for following behind her like a lost puppy, angry at Carter for telling me it's more than just a good fuck for him.

And now as I saw her taunting all of us, I realized how much I missed her. And not in a way that's appropriate for a stepfather.

I even tried to come clean to my wife, but as she always has been, she's busy. With herself. I don't know the reason to why we are still together, why she hasn't walked away. I'm good to her, I know that, but there isn't anything *real* between us.

There are moments, after she has had a few glasses of wine, she changes into this needy woman, but it seems Katie has cursed me and that I'm unable to *perform* anymore.

As I clean up the living room, I sigh. I shouldn't want my stepdaughter, especially not in front of my wife. Then again, I'm looking for any excuse to wait my wife out, so I don't have to tell some lie as to why I don't want to fuck the woman I'm supposed to love.

And then, as my wife goes upstairs, I find Katie's pink lacy bra stuffed under a pillow on the couch.

I stare at it, dangling from my finger. *They had her earlier.* That thought wiggles deeper and deeper into my head. *My sons had her, and I haven't.*

I saw her teasing them at dinner and how frustrated they were getting with her, but I also noticed the way she looked at me.

She's a greedy little whore.

But she's greedy for us.

I can't have her. Can't make her mine, but until she starts dating, leaves me, leaves *us* – something her mother is eager for – I'll have to get my fill of her. Make sure I'm a memory she can never erase.

Heading upstairs, I stare at the master bedroom, where I'm expected, and Katie's closed door.

Without a sound, I check on my wife, finding her asleep. My jaw ticks as I realize I'm losing. I close the door as a sigh leaves me. I pause, waiting for that voice inside my head to scream at me for doing this, for even thinking about it. But it doesn't come.

And I head to Katie's room.

I'll have to keep her quiet, not wanting anyone to walk in on us. This excitement grows, paired with this tickle of fear. Fear of being caught. My breathing is almost silent as I step through the doorway and close the door behind me. Stalking closer to the innocent angel sleeping. Carefully, I tug the flimsy sheet down and suck in a sharp breath as my eyes rake over her naked body. As if she knew I was coming to her, or is that wishful thinking?

My gaze travels over her sweet little cunt, her belly, her breasts, and I inch closer, gently stroking around one nipple, watching it pucker as she sighs.

I lean forward and lick over her nipple once. Her fingers curl, but that's it. I suck her nipple, flick my tongue over it, then push her thighs open. My cock twitches alive in my pants, and my hunger for her rises.

She moans softly, and I draw back. "Stay asleep, angel. You get to enjoy it tonight. You don't have to worry."

She settles back in as if my words are all she needs. I climb over her, settle between her legs, and free my painfully hard cock, rub it over her wet pussy as I switch to her other nipple, licking and swirling my tongue around the hard peak.

"Daddy will take care of his little whore." Leisurely, I nudge my cock against her pussy and then slide in. Feeling how her cunt wraps around me, gripping me deeper. "I missed you so much. Daddy's little whore."

Her lips part, her hips lift to take me better, and I grin.

She's so perfect for me. So damn eager for me.

I slip deeper until her tight pussy takes every inch. I draw back as I lean up, watching how pretty she looks with my cock inside her as I slowly ease out, then back in, over and over, nice and slow. I cup her breast, playing with her nipple as I increase the pace.

Katie quietly moans, and I quickly cover her mouth with my hand. Her warm breath rubs against my palm, and her eyes dart under her lids.

I can't resist this fucking temptation. I fuck her harder; the headboard squeaks and nudges against the wall.

"That's it, take Daddy's cock. You love it, don't you? Waking up with my cum on you," I groan.

She gasps, her hips rising against mine again. Her lips part against my hand, and it breaks me. I finish deep inside her, flooding her with my cum as my body twitches.

My chest heaves, and I move back, grinning while my cum leaks out of her, puddling between her legs and slicking her thigh.

Licking my lips, I keep my restraint, wanting her to find the *mess* I made. I gently kiss her forehead as I pull her sheet over her and set her bra over the headboard like a prize.

"Be a good girl tomorrow. No teasing. And pick up your clothes."

I linger there for a moment longer, watching her settle in, the flush on her face fading. "Such a naughty little angel. Tempting Daddy constantly."

Something shifts beside me, and I shake my head, knowing who lurks in the shadow.

"You weren't allowed to be with her," I say into the room.

"Allowed?" he laughs, stepping closer. "I can do everything I want."

Brad is the one who defies me at any moment he can, but this is different. He chose to stay with her, showing he cared more than he should. Even with all I tried, I couldn't persuade him to come home.

Maybe it wasn't Carter I should have worried about; perhaps it was Brad.

"She is just a good fuck, remember that," I whisper shout, but my words don't even convince me anymore. I didn't only miss that tight cunt of her, I missed *her*.

"She's the best fuck, one I'll have for the rest of my life," he says, moving into the soft light from outside. His joggers strained over his hard cock, and I shake my head again.

"Her mom won't agree with it."

He chuckles softly. "Who says I care?"

I nod to Katie. "She will."

# CHAPTER THIRTY

*Katie*

I squirm as the morning sun prickles my eyes, and I try to turn. But a strong arm is keeping me in place. The scent of cinnamon invades my senses, and I snuggle closer, knowing who's holding me tight.

As I feel the stickiness between my legs, my eyes slowly flutter open. Only Daddy fucks me in my sleep and leaves me a mess like this.

I breathe in relief. Relieved he still wants me, not even caring how wrong this all is.

Glancing up, I meet Brad's stare, sighing to himself as he looks at me. I bite my bottom lip as my smile threatens to widen.

"You still don't want me to sleep alone?" Sure, it was his excuse when we were at Harvard. He told me it wasn't safe to sleep alone and that someone could grab me, but he can't use that excuse anymore.

"Well, it's safer," he shrugs.

I chuckle softly and rest my head on his chest. "And you're protecting me from who exactly?"

He didn't keep Daddy off me, and I wonder if he joined. I shiver at the thought as heat courses under my skin.

He says nothing as his gaze rakes over my body, as if he knows what dirty thought is going through my mind.

His fingers slide down my body, brushing over my nipples, down my stomach and between my legs. He presses down on my clit, and I gasp.

"Make a sound, and I'll stop."

Pulling my lips behind my teeth, I swallow all the sounds that dare to surface. Not caring about the mess Daddy made, Brad teases lower. His finger works inside me while his thumb keeps grazing my clit.

"Don't push it," he warns as he toys with me further, with touches too soft to make me come but more than enough to make me crave him.

He adds another finger into my aching cunt while keeping his thumb on my clit. He fingers me hard and fast as I bite my bottom lip and cover my mouth while Brad's eyes stay focused on mine. "You're such a slut, letting me use you however I want, aren't you?"

I nod weakly, and with a wicked smile, he stops just like that.

I whimper and shake my head, pulling him closer. "Don't stop," I whisper.

His lips brush over my ear as he whispers, "You don't get to decide when I stop."

Brad covers my mouth with his hand, holding me down as he moves over me. "I'm going to edge you for as long as I want. Making you remember that *I* get to decide how you come."

He plunges his fingers inside me, hitting that sweet spot as he slowly tortures me, bringing me to the edge, as my hips buck for more and then he slows, luring me back as I wither beneath him, desperate for a release, he starts again.

Tormenting me with his touch, toying with my clit, my core pulses for more and I climb higher, balancing on that thin line and his touch fades.

He edges me again and again with his fingers, making me squirm and pant as his hot palm presses against my mouth. Tears roll down my cheeks and sweat paints my skin as I can't handle his plays.

"I *own* you. Remember that." He grits as my body spasms beneath his. "Come."

I bite back every moan as I come apart for his fingers, filling me perfectly, rubbing my G-spot and clit. I gush over his fingers, my juices coating his hand.

He jerks back after a second and pats my pussy. "That's how you be a good slut. Remember that."

I wipe away the tears, my body shaking with its release as Brad storms out. I hurt him somehow, and that's why he's doing this. Punishing me, making me remember how much control he has. But I don't get it, not yet.

He's different here, different than how he was at college, as if he's feeling insecure and had this need to prove to whom I belong.

But I already know that.

And then it hits me.

My mom and her words.

He fears he might lose me to someone else. I shake my head, crawling out of bed to get cleaned up. My legs are wobbly as I step into the bathroom and a soft smile plays on my lips.

Brad's jealous of the man I'll spend the rest of my life with.

However, he forgets one thing.

I don't believe I want anyone else besides *them*.

The scent of scrambled eggs surrounds me as I head downstairs. Carter is working on his laptop, his eyes glued to the screen. Brad is focused entirely on his phone, as if this morning didn't happen, and my step-dad is making breakfast.

Do they forget that easily or are they all that good at pretending?

My mom changes the channel on the TV and curls around her cup of tea. "What are you two up to?"

"Maybe some strolling through the woods," Brad says as his gaze cuts to me.

My mother takes a sip from her tea. "And you, Carter?"

"Ehm... I'm going with him," Carter mumbles as he types away on his laptop.

I ignore their conversation when I notice Daddy's alone in the kitchen, working hard on breakfast.

I say my good mornings, then head to the kitchen. I grab an apple from the island, my ass rubbing against Daddy's hip, and I hear him pause.

"Good morning," I hum softly.

"Is it?"

I grin over my shoulder at him, and he glances back, his eyes focused on my ass for a second before he goes back to his eggs.

I have to be twice as careful, considering my mom is sitting on the couch.

Not that her being here makes me want to stop. If anything, I want Daddy more. I want to prove that I can give him what he needs ... and I can do it awake as well as I can while asleep.

I hike my oversized dress higher, showing my lack of panties. I can be a good girl. I can be just what my stepbrothers and Daddy want.

"What are your plans today?" he asks casually.

"I don't have any," I reply.

"I'm glad to see you two getting along so well," Mom says with a beaming smile.

I smile back as I take another bite of the apple, and she returns her focus to the TV, sipping her tea easily.

"Actually, I might go out today," I say softly.

"Where?" My stepdad asks.

I bite my bottom lip. "Just out."

He narrows his eyes at me, but I glance at my mom, then sigh. "I'll be right back."

He watches as I sink to my knees and crawl over to him. He can't fuck me here, but I can take care of him without being seen.

"Hurry back for breakfast," Mom calls, without even noticing I never left.

"I'm eager for breakfast," I whisper.

"To fill your mouth," Daddy corrects, grabbing my hair tightly. "Did you ask permission?"

Keeping my voice in a low whisper while stroking through his pants, feeling how hard he is. "Please, Daddy?"

He continues watching me before I sigh. "Please, Daddy, let me suck your cock."

He nods and goes back to working on breakfast.

Slowly, I drag his zipper down, undo his button, and free his thick cock. I wrap my hand around the shaft, slowly stroking him until the head touches my lips. I lick across, hearing him take a shaky breath, and then I go for more.

My lips part further, wrapping around the tip, and I carefully push down. Taking every inch even slower than the one before. I gaze up, watching his jaw flex as I move back, sucking slightly and then letting him fill me again, pushing as far as I can take until I gag around him.

I bob on his cock, not daring to make a sound as my hand grazes lower, bundling the dress around my waist, making sure he sees my naked ass.

My thighs tremble, my pussy weeps for more and I suck harder.

"Honey, what time do you want to head to the store?" my mom asks my stepdad. He grips the kitchen island, on the verge of breaking as I pick up my pace, pushing his boundaries as my core coils.

"Whatever you want, dear," he manages to say, and my mom doesn't seem to notice the strain in his voice.

My fingers graze over his tight balls, and he hisses.

His hand comes down, curling around the back of my head as he takes over and fucks me deeper. Harsh and fast, punishing me the most he can.

He thrusts into my throat, his eyes flicking to me, and then he pushes in as deep as possible. I squirm and wither beneath him as I can't breathe.

"Fucking perfect," he groans as his cum fills me.

"What did you say, dear?" my mom asks.

"The eggs, they look perfect," he quickly says, and releases the back of my head.

I swallow every bit, licking his half-hard cock before I tug him back inside his pants and rise to my feet.

He reaches for me, brushing his thumb over my lip and dips it in my mouth. The salty taste of his cum moves over my tongue as I suck his finger clean and inch closer. His hand trails over my body, under my dress and between my legs.

He smiles and whispers. "All for me?"

I nod, and he lifts his fingers to his lips, sucking my moisture from them. "Delicious."

Christmas will be a whole lot of fun as long as Mom doesn't find out. This will be a very happy, very satisfying Christmas break.

# Chapter Thirty-One

B rad wasn't joking when he said to my mom he wanted to go on a stroll in the woods. And it seems, I had no other choice but to go with them.

And now as I sit in the backseat, staring out the window, my brows knit as I see we are leaving town.

"Where are we heading?" I ask.

"We are playing a game," Carter says.

"What game?" I ask.

Brad chuckles. "*My* game."

My face heats as memories of Brad following me through the forest surface. "What? Are you..." My words come out in stammers as my insides clench. Fear and excitement swirl around each other.

"If you get away, you get a prize. If you don't ..." his eyes stroke over me through the mirror. "I'm the one who gets to enjoy myself."

My thighs squeeze together and my breathing changes, my blood pumping faster as Brad stops at the side of the road, my eyes grazing over the woods in the distance. The trees reach high for the sky as snow covers the ground.

"Run. You get a ten-second head start," he says darkly.

I'm not sure what I want here. Do I want to win, or do I want to lose?

I leap out of the car, sprinting with all I have. My heart lodges in my chest, and I rip through the forest, not daring to glance back as I hear their boots hit the snow.

"Here we come," I hear, far too close to me.

For some reason, those three words spur me on. I try to hop over branches and soften my stride on the cold snow as I pant. The icy air burns my lungs, steals my energy, and I can see every quick breath I take.

"I'm getting closer, Katie. I think you want me to catch you, little slut," Brad sings.

I whimper and sprint, going as fast as my legs will carry me. I have to get away.

A branch cracks behind me, and I hide behind a tree. The thrill of being captured is softened by how fucking cold it is. My heart still pounds against my ribs as I hear Brad running.

"You leave a hell of a trail," he taunts. "Just wait until I catch you."

I grip the tree tightly.

"I'm going to throw you down and fuck you until people believe there's a wolf howling here instead of a little slut begging her stepbrother to fuck her raw and wild."

The excitement in his voice nearly draws me to him, but I run in the opposite direction.

The game doesn't last much longer. As I run, I feel eyes on me, then a warm breath on the back of my neck as a strong hand digs into my arm. "You're not fast enough, Katie."

He lifts me against a tree; his body wraps over me as he groans. "Are you that eager? It's only been ten minutes."

He's panting above me. Brad's voice is so dark, so vicious, fear takes a swipe at my chest. "But I know you want it. You're soaking wet, aren't you?"

"N-no!" I hiss.

He jerks my pants down and palms my ass. "Spread your fucking legs."

I squirm and wiggle, trying to get free until his cold hands slide between my legs and rub my clit. He groans. "Fucking dripping. You want it."

"I ..." Words fail me as my body won't stop shaking. I don't know if it's the cold of winter seeping in or how every word he says weighs on me as his body rubs against mine, his need fueling mine.

"That's right," he hisses as he opens his pants. "And you're going to get fucked right here, like an animal."

I whine, but he lifts my hips and thrusts inside me in one go. A sharp cry leaves me, and he grips my hair, jerking my head to the side to bite my throat.

"You are a little slut, moaning like that," he snarls as I moan and whimper under him.

My fingers curl, and my legs slowly rise, tugging him closer as he pounds into me ruthlessly.

"You're mine to use as I see fit," he continues, panting against my throat. "And you don't get to hide how much you want it. You are going to scream for me."

He reaches under my jacket and sweater and pinches my nipple hard. Nothing he does is gentle.

His hand knotted in my hair, jerking back so I can't hide the screams leaving my throat, the way he's thrusting inside me fast and deep, not caring what I need, just chasing his own pleasure.

His balls slap against my skin as he bottoms out, drawing another sharp scream from me.

It's so rough, so overwhelming, that I can't remember the difference between pleasure and pain.

"Let the whole world hear how much you like being caught and fucked," Brad taunts.

His hand drops from my nipple to my clit, teasing me as he plows me. "Come for me," he whispers, and I come crashing down, moaning his name as every bit of cold skin heats. He stills deep inside me as my pussy clenches around his cock, his cum spurting out as a low chuckle leaves him.

"She didn't get too far, brother." He lifts his head from the crook of my neck, and I follow his gaze.

Carter looks between us, panting, confused, but Brad chuckles. "She wants all of this."

Carter steps closer, a grin playing on his lips as he peels me from Brad, letting me fall to the ground, my knees hitting the snow, and I shiver as my bare pussy feels the chill.

Without a word, he grabs the nape of my neck and frees his cock, quickly thrusting it into my mouth. Muffling the moans that try to leave me as Brad lifts me on my knees, my ass curved back for him as he toys with my pussy.

"Such a good slut," he praises from behind me.

"You're not leaving until you make me come, doll," Carter snarls, pushing his cock further until I'm nearly choking. "And have taken me in every hole here in this forest."

"That is what you get with teasing us during dinner, thinking we wouldn't do anything. Did you really think we wouldn't punish you?" Brad asks.

Carter groans. "Just can't resist stealing our attention, goading us, working us up until we have to have you."

I can't handle them both, not like this, when they're so worked up and so damn eager. They push me near the edge again, my moans vibrating around Carter's pumping cock.

Carter grabs my cheeks, forcing them together. "Swallow every fucking drop."

My eyes are locked on him, as he pushes his cock deep down my throat; I swallow, my muscles working around his length as his cum drips down.

My cold fingers grip his hips tightly as my legs hurt from the cold. Brad's touch leaves me, and Carter slowly pulls out, but his wicked grin forces me to inch back.

"I don't think we've fucked her nearly enough," Carter says darkly.

"Is that so?" Brad lifts my chin. "Can you handle more, little slut?"

I nod, and my brows pinch.

"See, not nearly enough," Carter chuckles. "You want more doll? You're going to get it. But neither of us will be gentle."

# Chapter Thirty-Two

My steps are sloppy as the sun slowly sets, and the evening breeze chills me to my spine. I don't know what came over me, to think I could run from that again, but the pleased look on Brad's face when I did can't stop my smile.

I know how much he likes to chase and hunt, and I also know how much they both like me to struggle.

I should have paid more attention to where I was going because I feel like I'm walking in circles as I notice the trial of footsteps before me.

But as I place my foot into the mark in the snow, my brows knit, noticing it doesn't fit. I follow it, carefully, stepping in the footsteps of another, wondering where these will take me.

Every footstep is slow and cautious, never daring to step out of the marks in front of me. My heart rate slows, my breathing shallows as I listen to the sounds around me. The soft crunching of the snow beneath my boots, the wind that rustles through the trees, and then I hear something I shouldn't.

Voices.

Their voices.

I crouch down, shielding myself behind the trees as I inch closer, enough to glance past the tree bark.

"You got the same speech, right?" Brad asks Carter as he leans against a tree while balling some snow in his hands.

Carter huffs, his hands stuffed deep in his pockets as he shakes his head. "Of course, got it the moment I got home." He pauses as he looks up at Brad. "Are you going back with her again?"

"Back to college? Definitely!"

They both laugh as Brad is the first to toss the snowball at Carter.

"It surprises me that Dad didn't come to get you." Carter brushes the snow off his jacket as he lowers himself, grabbing some off the ground.

"Oh, he did," Brad says as he pushes himself off the tree. "He tried to get me back home, but it turned into a tiny fight." He shrugs as if it means nothing, but it does. I never knew my stepdad came for Brad and tried to take him away from me. My jaw ticks as anger bubbles inside me. How could he do that?

"He's scared, you know. Afraid that we love her and forget that this is just some itch."

My chest constricts as his words cut me. I try to shake it off and climb out of hiding.

"This isn't some itch, Brad," Carter says and stiffens slightly when he hears my steps in the snow.

"You two aren't even looking for me," I snap, crossing my arms as I tap my foot on the ground.

They both stare at me, a softness, a vulnerability shines in their eyes, just before it changed to what I'm used to. This hunger and need as they prowl closer, both letting the snow slip through their fingers as I walk back with lifted hands, telling them not to come any closer.

But since when do they listen.

Carter is the first to speak, "Don't look at me like that. You know I love you." He grabs my hand, pulling me hard against him as his other hand grabs my hair.

"And Brad, well, he has his own kind of love," Carter jokes as Brad moves behind me, the heat of their covert bodies' seeps into mine and the simmering anger fades into nothing.

"It seems our pet came crawling back herself, because we took too long," Brad taunts as he carefully tugs my pants down.

"No, that wasn't what I wa—"

"Oh, stop pretending. If you didn't want it, you would have hidden better," Carter says while shoving one hand under my shirt to palm my breast.

At the same time, Brad pushes his fingers between my legs, stroking and teasing me until I'm shaking. I can't pretend I don't want it, but I still push at Brad and Carter's hands on me. Trying to fight in their grasp.

Carter tightens his hold on my wrist, holding it above my head while Brad jerks my hair back. "Behave, little slut."

"It's too cold!" I complain. "And I didn't...aah."

Brad bites my neck hard, and I cry as Carter manages to snare my free arm, keeping both my wrists hostage in his firm hand. I gasp and tug, but he holds my hands in the air so high, I end up standing on my toes.

Brad thrusts his fingers inside me. "Your pussy is soaked whenever you see us."

I whimper and squirm as his fingers follow my ass, readying me for what's to come. "Spread your legs, little slut."

"Now," Carter agrees, glowering at me while bunching my top up over my breasts and tugs my nipple.

I don't obediently obey and Brad groans, thrusting a finger into my ass. He spreads my legs with his foot, bends me slightly with Carter's help, then his cock nudges against my ass, stretching me, inch for inch as I cry.

"Is this what you were fishing for? You wanted us to be even rougher, little slut?" Brad snarls, sliding his cock completely inside me.

"Moan for him, Doll," Carter orders, pinching and turning my nipple again.

I can't think, I can't breathe. Brad's cock pumping inside my ass, the pain of Carter's fingers on my breast. I moan and squirm until Carter swats my breast. "Too loud, as always."

"I'm sure you have a way to shut our girl up, don't you?" Brad says between thrusts. "I don't think she wants anyone to find out what she allows her stepbrothers to do to her. What she goads us into doing to her."

"Please." I don't know what I'm begging for but that doesn't matter. Not when Carter frees his cock, then shoves it into my empty pussy.

My eyes water as he thrusts all the way in, and lifts one leg around his hips while releasing my wrists. I don't know if I'm going to die or come, but both feel possible right now. Not a sound leaves me as my body shakes between them.

"Take us both. I know how you like it."

I don't want to like it, not when they're this rough, but I do. It doesn't matter what it says about me. I'm greedy to have them like this, both of them taking me like they need me specifically, like they know I can handle their darkest fantasies and like it as much as they do.

"Do you want my cum?" Carter snarls.

I nod as best I can as Brad's hand snakes between Carter and me and plays with my clit.

They own me. I'm theirs entirely. I don't know why I ever thought I could leave them, why I'd wanted to. I moan and pant, trying to hold on, trying to squirm, to get them where I need, but before I can even get myself ready, my orgasm curls my toes.

My skin heats, making me forget about the icy breeze that tickles over me.

Brad groans, his thrusts becoming sloppy as his cock hardens further. "Come, little slut. Before I finish in your ass."

"Better hurry. If you don't come first, you're not going to come at all," Carter hisses. "Maybe you shouldn't. You should be frustrated until we have you again."

Those words shouldn't make me insane, but they do. I fall over the edge and into an orgasm just as Brad stills inside me, filling my ass with his cum.

My eyes flutter closed, as my body and soul are exhausted.

But I'm with my guys, and I know I'm safe.

That's good enough.

# Chapter Thirty-Three

I stir in my bed as my eyes slowly flutter open. Wait, how did I get home? I was in the woods... My thoughts stop as my body twitches, and then I feel it, the soft nibbles, the licks and plays. I moan, my back arches as he sucks on my clit.

Dipping my hands under the cover, my fingers rake through his thick hair, and I tug him closer.

"Daddy," I moan, knowing exactly who wakes me like this.

He groans and sucks on my clit.

"Fuck," I hiss, my hips bucking against him as his grip on my legs tightens.

He releases my clit with a pop. "You were very bad yesterday. Sucking me off while your mom sat a few feet away from us." He groans, the tip of his tongue flicks over my clit, and then wanders lower to my entrance.

"I should punish you for it," he teases as his tongue thrusts inside me.

"Please, please do."

He freezes, and so do I, as he doesn't say anything. The sheet that kept him hidden slowly falls off him as he crawls up my naked body.

"What did you say?" he asks, his eyes burning in mine. "You want me to punish you? To slap your ass so hard that you beg me to stop, is that what you want?"

My chest heaves, and my perked nipples brush over his skin. "Yes," I breathe.

He doesn't say anything and rolls off me, grabbing his robe and leaving me without a word.

Shit. Did I say the wrong thing? But I thought nothing was off-limits.

My eyes prickle as I get out of bed, grabbing some clothes to get ready for my shopping trip today. I shouldn't let it get to me, right? I shouldn't let his rejection pain me so much, but it does. My heart stammers, my ribs tighten as my breathing shallows.

As I tiptoe downstairs, hoping to see him, to see my stepdad, but he isn't there. Only my mother sits on the

couch with her magazines and tea, just like yesterday when I sucked her husband behind the kitchen
counter.

I gulp, realizing how messed up I am, how messed up
this situation is. Everything.

But the thought of it stopping, hurt me the most. I
can't have what my mom has, and if I tell her what I
want, I will only hurt her.

With a deep sigh, I slump beside her. "Where's Dad?"
I try to keep the shiver from my voice as she glares at me.

"He's probably getting some presents or something."
She smiles sweetly, her eyes glinting with happiness, and
it only adds to that harsh sting in my chest.

"Are you happy with him?" Fuck, why did I ask that?
Do I even want to know that?

Her brow twitches, and her head tilts slightly. "Why
do you ask, sweetie?"

"Just checking if you're happy."

She takes my hand, squeezing it gently. "I am, don't
you worry. He's a good man, the best I can wish for."

Oh, crap.

"He likes you very much, too," she says when I don't
respond.

"I like him too," I say, even though I know it's turning
into something more.

I thought I only cared for Brad and Carter in that way, but after what happened upstairs, I fear my feelings are more than I thought.

"Sweetie, is it true that Brad stayed with you?" Her grip on my hand tightens and a blush reddens my cheek. How could I even think she wouldn't find that out? Daddy knew.

"Sort of," I pause as she watches me closely. "It was nice having him around."

She hums, her fingers peel from my hand. "Be careful with him, I don't want you to get in... trouble."

"Trouble?" I ask, maybe a tad too quick.

"I don't know everything, of course. But Henry had to bail him out a few times, but he wouldn't tell me for what."

"I'm sure it was nothing, and if it were, Dad would have told you."

She nods with a hum, focusing back on her magazines, and my eyes dart behind her, locking with Carter's.

"I'm going to the mall. Do you need anything?" I ask my mom as I get up.

"No, I'm good," she says without even a glance.

I smile at her, and walk toward Carter, tugging him around the corner to the hallway.

"What don't I know?" I whisper shout as Carter tucks his phone in his back pocket.

"How do you think Brad got so good at chasing you in the woods?" He tilts his head, his eyebrow raises, and I shake my head.

"He ra—" I can't say it.

"Did we rape you?"

"I don't see it like that now, but I did when it happened." My voice is low, unsure if I even should say it.

"I would do it again." He inches closer and I step back until I hit the wall. "I would even be rougher, fuck you harder, make you cry as I'm buried deep inside you."

My breath catches, and his fingers graze over my chin as he leans closer. "I can even fuck you now, right here, while your mom sits on the other side of this flimsy wall."

"Carter," I breathe as his hand dips lower, nudging inside my pants.

"What did we say?" he shakes his head, unbuttoning my jeans and pushing it down.

"Only dresses," I respond. "But I was going to the sto—" I swallow my last words as two fingers thrust inside me.

I hold onto his shoulder tightly, as he pumps inside me, stretching me as his cock grows.

"Always ready for me, aren't we doll?" he chuckles, his fingers leaving me and then he turns me, pressing my face against the wall as he unzips his pants, taking out his cock and nudging in between my legs.

"Tell me again how I raped you," he taunts and glides inside me.

My hips tilt as a breathy moan falls from my lips.

"Tell me to stop now, tell me I should go back home and never touch you again."

Clenching my eyes shut, I shake my head. "Don't stop, never stop," I plead.

He chuckles softly, thrusting harder inside me. The picture frames to my right slightly move from impact and I fear one might fall.

"Careful now, we don't want your mom walking in on us." His fingers grip my hips almost painfully as he thrusts slow but hard and deep. As he hits that sweet spot deep inside me, pleasure shoots through my body, my walls wrapping around his cock, forcing a groan from his throat.

"How can something so wrong, feel so good," he whispers as his lips hover over my ear.

"Tell me you want this," he orders, my legs trembling, strength leaving as I'm ready to come.

He doesn't soften his pump, neither does his grip, torturing me with touches, with his cock, bringing me on the verge of climaxing.

"I want this," I moan. "All of this."

"Show me, show me how good you come over my cock," he grits. His touch, his words, the way he looks at me, it shatters me from the inside out, craving more every time.

A muffled cry resonates from me as my pussy spasms, milking his cock while I come undone over his thrusting cock and pants.

Not a sound leaves us, nothing other than our sharp intakes of air as he slowly and carefully peels himself away from me, taking his warmth with him.

I look down and I shimmy my pants back up as his slick cum drips down.

His fingers hook under my chin, and he tilts my head up. "You are all I want, Katie. Remember that."

"I know."

He shakes his head. "I don't think you do. I don't think you understand what I'm feeling." His jaw tenses as his gaze falls and he carefully peels himself away from me.

"Come, grab your shoes. I'll take you to the mall."

I slip on my shoes, my mind a whirlwind of conflicting emotions.

As we leave, I steal a glance at my mother, still reading her magazines, oblivious to what just happened.

# Chapter Thirty-Four

The drive over to the mall was in silence, a slightly uncomfortable one. But I wasn't the only one to blame. Carter was on his phone the entire drive, typing away as if he was in some kind of argument, and when I asked him about it, he only smiled and said it was nothing I should concern myself with.

And now as the Uber driver stops in front of the mall entrance, I hop out of the car, trying to ignore the sticky wetness between my legs. My jeans aren't helping a thing. Every time the seam of my pants rubs against my pussy, and not in a good way. I should have changed or taken a quick shower, but Carter almost pushed me out of the house.

Carter glances at me and chuckles. "Something wrong, Doll?"

"No," I answer softly, ignoring the fact that half the wetness I feel is him. "I'm just thinking about Christmas things."

He edges closer, his body brushes against my back as he tilts his head lower. "Sure, you are. You're not thinking about fucking so close to mommy dearest and wondering if she heard what we were doing but is nice enough not to say anything," he grunts in my ear and a shiver rakes through my spine.

As a blush reddens my cheeks, I step away from him. "Stop taunting me," I whisper shout and pick up my pace, needing some distance between us.

With his phone back in hand, he catches up and intertwines his fingers with mine. Seeming like a normal couple strolling through the mall. The Christmas decorations fill the large space, the soft music that plays in the background. But what I see the most, are the looks. The eyes of people we know.

"Carter," I say, and he focuses back on me.

"What's wrong?" he asks as tension builds in my body. My heart stammers in my chest as I don't know what to do. I shouldn't care, I know that. But now, with my mom at home, I do. I don't want her to find out from somebody else.

"I-I need to get you a present, so you can't come with me." I muster a smile as I meet his eyes, and he slowly nods.

"Fine, text me when you're done." He pulls me closer; his lips find mine and the tension intensifies.

He smiles against my lips and whispers, "Let them watch, Katie."

My shoulders drop as I let myself get lost in the feeling he gives me. The safety and love.

"Good girl," he says as our lips part.

I grin at him and move away, leaving him so I can do what I came here for. Because what do I give them when they have everything they want?

I check a few stores for the guys. Wondering if I should get something for Carter's work, or his home in London. And then Brad, what could I give him?

My mind is in turmoil as I try to come up with the best gift possible and then I spot a lingerie store. I shouldn't go in. I should behave, but the temptation to be naughty is impossible to ignore.

I go in and try to ignore all the sex toys as I head to the lingerie instead. I don't need to look. I have more than enough to take care of my urges. Three men willing to enjoy me, to push every button and then some. How can I possibly want anything more than that?

I touch some of the lacy fabrics, the fish nets, the silk.

"That's a good one. Your boyfriend will love it," the shop worker says.

I thank her and try a few things on. I still can't imagine wearing anything like this. But then I think about all the bad things I've done so far. There's too many to count. Wearing lingerie should be nothing in comparison to being hunted down in the woods and fucked hard.

I chew my bottom lip and get three different outfits. One is frilly and pink, almost innocent, if it didn't push my boobs up instead of covering them up and wasn't a barely there crotchless thong type thing. Perfect for Daddy when he sneaks into my bedroom at night.

Then a little black lacy dress that wouldn't hide a thing. I'm sure Brad will love tearing it off me.

Carter's the hard one. Nothing bothers him more than a challenge so I get something I can't even figure out how to put on. The red straps cling to my body, shielding all he likes. It's tight and gives him his challenge, the one he craves the most.

I'm still blushing when I check out even though the woman says 'Merry Christmas' like a promise with a wink to go with it.

I wander around the mall, getting the ingredients to make some gingerbread cookies this afternoon and try to find something perfect for my mom. It won't matter, though. She never held onto a present for longer than a few months. Hell, I've seen the stuff that she regifts, pretending it's nothing at all.

After going in and out of stores, I huff and sit on the edge of a fountain, watching other people shop. Plenty of couples holding hands, happy families talking about the holiday without any obligation between them.

Huffing, I grab my phone, ready to text Carter. Just before I can hit send, I see Daddy.

He has some bags in his hands, and I run after him. I don't want to yell 'daddy' or 'stepdad' across the mall, and I can't seem to get close enough to grab him either.

As I follow him to the parking lot, I almost yell, but he tosses the bags in his car and gets in without looking my way.

"Daddy, wait, I want to talk about—"

The car starts and off he goes.

How the hell am I supposed to figure out what I did wrong with him if he won't talk to me? Did Mom say something to him? Does he want me to hate being punished? I don't get it. I need him to tell me why he pulled away this morning so I can fix it.

Sucking my bottom lip, I text Carter that I'm done shopping. He's quick with his reply and says he needs some more time. All I can do is wait and think, definitely not a great combination, but I don't know what else to do with myself, so I overthink my lingerie, my life, and the men I'm not supposed to want.

# CHAPTER THIRTY-FIVE

In just a few hours we have our Christmas dinner, and I can't wait to give my presents.

Excitement swirls inside me as the scent of freshly baked gingerbread cookies fills the open kitchen and living room, and I quickly make the final tweaks to the garland above the mantel.

My mom is leaving me to the decorations as she runs out to get some last-minute stuff at the mall. God knows what because I truly believe we already have everything we need.

Excitement grows inside me as I hear the rumbling of Brad's truck. I leap to the door, opening it with a swing, just in time as Brad hauls the tree out the back and heads toward me.

The fabric of his plated jacket clings to his arms as he groans loudly, bringing the tree inside.

Tossing the door closed, I quickly move around him without a word and grab the stand, securing the bottom of the tree before he puts it beside the fireplace in the corner of the living room.

Sweat drips off his forehead, and he wipes it away with the back of his hand as he takes a sharp breath.

"Those bastards let me do it alone," he grumbles with a shake of his head.

I have no idea where Carter and my stepdad are, usually all three of them go out for a tree.

"You're not alone anymore." I smile and open one of the boxes on the couch to start decorating the tree.

He smiles back, the tension in his shoulder drops, and he edges closer. "Just you and me?" Tilting his head slightly, his eyes rake over my body but stop at my belly as he sees what's on my Christmas sweater.

He chuckles and grabs the hem. "Where did you find this one?"

"Don't you like it?" I tease, glancing down at my old, oversized Christmas sweater with a red fluffy ball in the center that is supposed to be Rudolf's nose.

He steps closer with a small smile. "It looks great."

The scent of pine and fir wafts around me, and I peek up, edging closer until I feel his lips brush past mine.

"Kiss me," I whisper as he doesn't move.

His warm hand snakes beneath my red sweater and brushes around my waist as his lips press on mine.

There is a softness in his touch and lips, one I felt a few times when he followed me around college, one that's telling me this has become so much more than an easy fuck.

As our lips part and our foreheads rest against each other, something starts nagging inside me. The things my mom and Carter said about Brad.

With a sharp breath, my grip tightens on his arms. "I'm not your first."

He tenses as he leans back. "What do you mean?"

My fingers lose their grip as I regret my words. "Well, just something about what my mom said. That you... got arrested a few times."

"Why do you think I got arrested?" He stares me down as my heart begins to pick up its pace.

"I know what kind of *things* you like, so maybe it had something to do with that," I say carefully.

"I've had girlfriends before, you know that."

"I know, but how did that make you end up in jail."

He grins as his eyes darken. "You know how rough I can be, and sometimes we got caught. That's it, Katie. Nothing to worry about."

I gulp and nod. "I wasn't worried."

"Jealous that I played with someone else before you?"

Bastard. My eyes narrow as I huff. "No, of course not."

Amusement glints in his eyes. "You might not be my first, but you're my last."

"Your last?"

"Yes, little slut. Somehow, you won our little game, and now I can't stay away."

My face heats as his words register. I always thought he cared for me, even when he tried to hide it. "So, you do like me more than just a fuck."

He laughs as he shakes his head. "No, I don't."

My brows pinch as he moves closer and cups my face between his hands.

His jaw clenches as his eyes shift between mine and my lips. "I fucking love you, Katie."

My lips part, trying to find some words to speak, and he quickly presses his on mine. The gentleness from before has faded as he forces me back, nibbling on my bottom lip to respond and then I do. My lips follow his as he devours me, tasting me as his hands roam over my body, in search of my skin.

The buzzing of his phone pulls him away as he curses under his breath. With a sharp tone he picks up, but the anger softens just as quickly.

"Really?" he says, and I edge closer. A smile tugs on his lips, and I'm eager to know why that is.

He hums as his gaze cuts to me, warning me to stay put.

"Okay, great. See you in a bit." And with that he hangs up.

"Dad?" I ask as I still haven't talked to him since he ran out on me.

Brad shakes his head. "No, Carter. Just something about your Christmas gift."

My brow rises as I tilt my head. "And?"

"Nothing." He shrugs and grabs a box with ornaments from the couch. The warmth and joy are shielded behind his stoic layer, but I know better now. I recognize that small glint in his eyes, that whatever he and Carter are planning will change so much.

As we sift through boxes of ornaments, Brad holds up a delicate deformed glass ornament. "Look at this." He laughs softly, his eyes sparkling with nostalgia. "I believe this was one you made when we had our first Christmas together."

He dangles the ornament gently in front of me.

"Oh, god. It's awful." The self-made ornament should look like a reindeer but came out as a deformed brown mess. I shake my head as Brad carefully hangs it in the center.

"No, please, just hide it in the back, my mom will have a fit if she sees it." As I step closer, trying to reach for it to protect it from my mom's glare, Brad grabs my wrist, pulling me flush against him.

He inhales deeply as he lowers his lips to my ear. "Let it be, Katie. This Christmas isn't about her."

"Then what's it about?" I stare up at him, my cheeks heating.

"Us, only us."

I gulp and slowly nod.

We take turns hanging ornaments and sharing stories behind each one. A snow globe from Brad's first winter vacation, a quirky handmade ornament from a craft fair he attended with Carter when he was younger, and a tiny-framed photo capturing a special moment from our first Christmas as a family.

Until there is one left. Well, there are more, all the perfectly golden balls that my mom always wants me to use, but this year, the tree is filled with memories.

With the golden star in hand, standing on his toes, Brad carefully places the star at the very top, crowning the tree.

The room falls into a hushed stillness as he steps beside me, admiring our work. The tree sparks with our memories. Each ornament has its own story. Gently, I lean against him as his arm nudges me closer.

The lights cast a warm glow around us as Brad whispers, "Merry Christmas, Katie."

"Merry Christmas, Brad."

# Chapter Thirty-Six

This is it. Pretending I don't like the men around the table more than I should.

With a slight tremble in my hands, I smooth out my deep green dress. It's pretty and hints a little towards sexy, but it's appropriate enough to wear in front of my mother. I know there is nothing to be nervous about, but I can't shake this feeling that something is about to happen.

A shaky breath leaves me as I head downstairs. My heels clicking off the wooden stairs as I hold onto the banister tightly. My brown hair flows down my shoulders as I reach the hall. A smile threatens to form when I hear my stepbrothers' voices.

I peek around the corner and step inside the living room, my gaze falling on them. Both are wearing a red Christmas sweater, but this unease inside me still won't drop.

Clearing my throat, I smile and see my mom, her friend, and ... and a man my age. He has wavy blonde hair, a surfer-like attitude and is here. Why? Wait, what is happening?

"There you are, honey. Oh, you look beautiful," my mom says before taking my hand tightly and dragging me to the dining table. "You look much better than how you did with the Christmas tree." She sighs as her grip tightens, warning me that this won't be the end of it.

My stepdad takes a long drink of eggnog and shakes his head while looking away.

Mom whispers in my ear. "Good choice on the dress. Wyatt here is so excited to meet you, and I've been talking you up."

"Why?" I hiss, unable to hide the poison from my word.

But she doesn't feel it, doesn't respond to it as she ushers me to sit beside Wyatt.

"Katie, this is my friend Amelia and her son Wyatt. Wyatt, this is my charming daughter, the one I've been gushing about. She's as smart as she is beautiful. Don't you think she looks amazing in this dress?"

Wyatt gives me a long once over that does absolutely nothing for me. If Carter had given me a look like that, I know he'd have his hands under my dress in a second. If Brad had looked at me that way, 'perfect little slut' would have followed, and he would have asked how I planned to run in my heels.

"She does look amazing," Wyatt says with a smile.

"I think red would look better," Brad says, barely keeping a growl out of his voice.

Oh, I'm going to get punished. I'm sure of that. Even though I haven't done anything but dress up and show up to this stupid dinner.

I suck my bottom lip and try to ignore the fact that my mom is actively trying to sell me to Wyatt.

I know that's not *really* what she's doing, but that's what it feels like. She's trying to get Wyatt to want me by listing off all the good things.

"Of course, she comes with two protective older brothers," Mom says with a laugh.

"Stepbrothers." I keep my ankles crossed under the chair, not knowing what else to do with myself. Mom and, Amelia and Wyatt are the only ones talking. I'm afraid to even look at Brad, Carter, or Daddy. I don't want to see their faces. Not with all this going on, and I can't stop the slight prickle burning my eyes.

"She always says that." Mom laughs lightly. "So, Wyatt, are you going to college close by or..."

"I graduated last year, so I'm living here, working here. I feel pretty stable and set," he answers, then looks at me. "What do you want to do with your future, Katie?'

"Oh, I want to—"

"She's still debating her options, you know?" my mom says, nudging my shoulder. "Isn't he cute?"

"Mom," I hiss once again.

"And Katie here is very excited to embrace the world and all the possibilities, you know? I'm sure all she needs is a special man in her life and—"

"Mom," I try again.

"I'm just saying, you're not getting any younger, honey, and Wyatt here is attractive and obviously interested. It wouldn't be long-distance for long and—"

"I have a boyfriend!" I blurt out, silencing the entire table. No forks scrape, no one sips, no one breathes. Their eyes are all on me, burning my skin.

Wyatt blinks a few times and shrugs. "This food is excellent, really great, and you guys are clearly a close family, which is ...uhm... great."

My mom stares at me. "Who? You haven't told me about anyone, and I asked! If you're making it up just to—"

"Don't do this. I'm taken," I say softly, keeping my eyes down.

I can't look at anyone. My eyes are dying to flick to my stepbrothers'. I want to take Brad's hand because he's right here next to me. I want him to speak up, to say something. I want Carter to say that Wyatt couldn't handle me anyway. I want my stepdad to say that we can move on since I'm clearly not comfortable.

No one's coming to the rescue, though. There's just me, standing utterly alone with a lump growing in my throat.

"Who are you dating?" Mom asks, cutting through her friend trying to say something. "Or are they made up?"

I scoff, blinking away the threatening tears and look up. "I'm not making up a boyfriend!" I grit.

"Who is it? We're all dying to know. The table's yours," my mother says sharply.

I swallow, my confidence wavering. "Brad," I whisper, sure that no one but Brad, sitting next to me hears it.

He freezes, not even breathing as he glares at me.

"What?" My Mom asks. "No one can hear you and if you have to whisper—"

"I'm dating ... Brad," I finally say.

I look over the table. All eyes go to Brad except Carter's. He looks at me before looking away, rubbing his jaw. I swallow. I know I just hurt him. I can see it etched onto his features even though he tries to hide it.

"Brad?" My Mom asks, barely softening her frustration. "Brad at this table right now, Brad?"

"Yes," I say, nearly choking on the word.

"Well ... this has been ... we're going to leave," Amelia says, clearly uncomfortable with the knowledge of me dating my stepbrother.

My Mom doesn't say anything as Amelia gestures to her son to get up from his chair.

"This has been... lovely," Wyatt says with a laugh and rises from his chair. The scratching on the floor is all the sound I hear as he follows his mom.

It doesn't take long before I hear the front door opening and closing as a starting sound for what's to come.

The talk I dreaded and feared.

"Are you kidding me! You're dating your stepbrother?!" My Mom seethes, her hands turning white as she grips her knife and fork harder.

"I ... it just happened, I didn't plan for it, but ... kind of?" I struggle.

"It just happened. How the hell does something like that just happen?" she yells while I just sit there, trying not to shake, trying to calm myself down, especially when Brad reaches out for me, taking my hand in his.

"Henry!" Mom yells. "What do you think about this? Huh? Give her a piece of your mind!"

Slowly, my eyes go to Daddy. He takes another drink and shrugs. "It's fine."

Mom's mouth opens, and she takes an unsteady breath. "Are you both sure about this?"

"Yes," I say.

Brad squeezes my hand. "Wouldn't be doing this if I wasn't sure."

"And you're happy?" she asks.

I nod. "Yes."

"Why wouldn't she be?" Brad asks.

My stepdad had to know this was coming. We couldn't keep all these secrets in one house. It's just not possible.

Mom sighs. "I can't believe you are dating your brother."

"There's more," I say while closing my eyes.

"What do you mean?"

"C-Carter," I finally answer. "I'm also with Carter."

# CHAPTER THIRTY-SEVEN

The silence is deafening. I want to scream just to put an end to it. My Mom jumps up, her hands banging down on the table. "Are you fucking kidding me, Katie!"

"Mom, I—"

"What kind of tramp sleeps with her brothers?! What kind of ... you can't just *date* them! Both of them?! How did any of this start!"

"Stepbrothers," I sigh as she continues.

"How have I ... what the hell have you three been doing in this house!" she screams.

I'm sure even the neighbors know what's going on at this point, and I want to sink into the floor. Brad tightens his grip on my hand. He doesn't like yelling, especially not when it's focused on me.

"Did they take advantage of you?! Did they force you? Huh?" My mother demands, obviously seeing red. "Both of you are going to get kicked out of the—"

"They didn't force me!" I insist, stopping her words. "I wanted everything."

"I told you about Brad's past and you still fell for him."

"Do you really think this happened yesterday?" I ask. "I wouldn't say I was in a relationship with them if it was one night, but—"

"Henry, say something!" Mom demands.

He takes a slow breath. "Let's all calm down and have a rational conversation about this. It involves the family as much as ... you three."

"You don't even look surprised!" Mom accuses, then horror etches across her face. "You knew about this!"

"Look, honey," Daddy tries to say.

"How could you keep this from me?! How could all of you know about this and not say a word?!" She demands. "Carter, say *something*!"

"I'm crazy about her and having her away at school nearly killed me," he answers.

Something about those words open something hot and needy inside me. I squirm. Carter looks over my dress and the corner of his mouth twitches up. His rule about dresses is upheld and he loves it.

"You said you didn't have a boyfriend!" my mother starts again.

"I know. I didn't want you to know yet. But I don't want to be tossed at some stranger like I'm nothing at all! Like I'm just some daughter you're trying to marry off, so I'm not in your hair anymore," I say, losing my temper.

"How dare you! That's not what I was doing."

"Katie," Brad says gently.

"Doll, let's all stay calm with this," Carter agrees.

I take a shaky breath as my mother's gaze cuts through my soul. "You're acting like a slut. You know that? You can't have two men!"

*Oh, if only she knew.*

"And to think that *you* knew about this all along, Henry! You didn't put up a fight, you didn't tell me, and you clearly didn't stop this!" Mom shouts.

Daddy adjusts in his seat and clears his throat. "I was clear to both boys, but I don't own them or force them in any way. I tried to deal with Brad when he went with Katie to college. I kept Carter from going, but I can only do so much. If they all care about each other, there is nothing I can do."

"And you're just accepting it?" Mom yells. "Do I mean anything to you at all?"

"Do I?" I demand. "Because you might actually know about this, have an idea about this, if you'd actually step up and be a mother instead of just some person I see occasionally!" I'm done. I know I should stay calm, but she can't sit here and yell at me because of my choices.

"Don't you take that tone with me! You lost the right to do that when you started sleeping with your stepbrothers!" Mom shrieks. "And *you*! Henry, if you can't even tell me about things like this – things happening in our own home – then I don't know what we're doing."

"Kids, make yourself scarce," he says with a deep undercurrent that promises no joy on this Christmas Eve.

I swallow and head upstairs quickly. Brad and Carter both join me, and Brad shuts the door dutifully. It doesn't keep out the yelling. I suck in deep breaths as I sit down on the bed and hold my head in my hands. "Please tell me that was the right thing to do."

"I'm not sure what else you could have done to avoid being tossed at that asshole, doll," Carter says, but he doesn't look at me.

"Are you mad at me too?" I ask softly. "I messed everything up. With Mom, Daddy, you guys."

I realize how badly I'm shaking. I know how I feel about them, and I certainly know how they think about me. I tremble again, worrying about the fallout of all this and if I'm even close to capable of handling the fallout, the reality, or anything in between.

"I was mad," Carter says. "But not at you, doll."

"If your mother dares call you a slut again, I'll have more than one problem with her," Brad growls. "Ruining my nickname for you just like that."

We still hear the shouting from downstairs, no matter how muffled it is. I can't make out the words, but I *know* that it's not going well. I hate that I'm the reason they're fighting.

"Hey, Katie," Brad says. "Take a breath."

"This is my fault, isn't it?" I ask softly.

"Listen here," Carter agrees, meeting my eyes. "What we did was our choice as much as yours, maybe more than yours. Same with Dad. You didn't cause that mess down there. If your mother hadn't tried to push you into someone else's arms, we wouldn't have had a problem."

"That doesn't make me feel better right now," I whisper.

"No, and it's a shame that we can't use other means to distract you," Brad hums. "*Our* little slut deserves to be reminded it's a good thing to have that title."

"And here she went and claimed us," Carter agrees, his lips ghosting across my neck. "Does that mean you're tossing Daddy to the wolves?"

"I don't ..." I can't think when they're touching me. "There's too much to think about right now."

"Then don't think, Katie," Brad says as he drags my skirt up my thighs. "You have the two of us right here. You shouldn't be thinking about a single thing."

"Nothing except us, since we're right here, all in your bed," Carter growls. "Our sweet little doll."

For the first time, I don't want them to turn off my brain or distract me. I stand up and walk away, rubbing my forehead before slipping out of my heels. The yelling becomes louder and then there's a door slam followed by silence.

Mom ran away. I'm sure of it.

I just broke apart my family because I've been with all the men in this house. Keeping it a secret was one thing, but now that it's been exposed, who knows what's coming.

# CHAPTER THIRTY-EIGHT

Why did I believe this all was a good idea? Because we all know this can't work.

"I shouldn't have said anything," I mumble. "If I just waited, sat it out, then after Christmas break, everything would have gone back to normal."

"Normal?" Carter asks, gripping my hand. "You think I would let you go again and be alone with Brad while I'm not there." He scoffs.

"Then what?"

He glances at Brad, a grin forming on both their faces, and I rip my hand free.

"What did you two do?" I cross my arms, my brows knit together as they continue to have their silent conversation.

"You tell her," Brad says and flops back on my bed.

"Tell me what!" My eyes cut at Carter who takes some keys from his back pocket.

"I'm not going back to London. I'm coming with you and Brad, to our new place."

"Wait what?"

"We bought an apartment for us to make our home, while you finish college," Brad says.

"Where we will live, together?" I ask carefully.

"Together," Carter repeats and peels my tensed arms from my body. "All three of us."

Tears fill my eyes, and quickly roll down my cheeks. This is it, right? We are doing this. All of us. Well...

"And what about...Henry?" I ask, purposely using his name.

Brad sighs and stands up. "I don't know, Katie. But we are staying with you. Forever."

He takes my hand from Carter and presses it on his chest. The steady beating of his heart pushes back. "My heart only beats for you."

I blink, staring at my hand as my breathing slows. His words burn into my soul as I realize what all this means. We can have a relationship, even with the twisted kinks, we can be everything.

Carter huffs and shoves Brad back. "Smooth," he jokes.

My tears dry as they both laugh, making me forget about all the troubles that await me downstairs and show me what we can have. *Together.*

"Doll, do you get a present for us?" Carter teases.

I say nothing as I move toward my closet, grabbing the bag stuffed in the bottom drawer and take out the two small intimate presents.

"I can never give what you two are giving me, so it might be a little silly," I say, handing them their small gifts.

Brad doesn't wait and rips it open, a smile spreads on his face as he dangles the flimsy black lace dress from his fingertips. "Oh, my little slut." He groans as his gaze cuts to mine.

Carter is gentler, peeling the tape from the wrapping paper and revealing the red contraption he would have to struggle around to get what he wants. "Oh doll, you're giving us *you*. That's all we want," he says as mischief roams in his gaze.

"We can share, right?" Brad says and quickly grabs the red strapped outfit. "How will this one work?"

I grin and step closer, hooking my finger under a red strap. "Let's find out."

Carter is quick, hauling me up and tossing me over his shoulder as he storms out of my bedroom and down the stairs. Panic sets in my stomach as I squirm in his grip. "Carter, where are you taking me!"

"Come on, doll. You and Brad made such a pretty tree, and it would look even better with you all wrapped in that red outfit in front of it."

My eyes widen as he steps into the living room. But when I peek around, there is no one here. Not my mom, not Henry.

I'm relieved but there is this small bit of me that is disappointed that *he* isn't here.

"Don't pout, little slut. He'll come back eventually," Brad says tugging on my bottom lip before Carter drops me in front of the tree.

With the contraption still hooked around my fingers, Carter hints toward it and shoves Brad out of the room.

I chuckle and slowly, peel my green dress from my body, removing my bra next and wrap the red lingerie around my body – even though I'm not sure it even qualifies as lingerie, considering how little fabric there is and how it twists around my body – I lay on the floor in front of my stepbrothers ... boyfriends? Oh, who cares, I'll figure out the words later.

They watch me with so much hunger, so much frustration, that I don't know why they're bothering to wait.

"Roll over," Carter orders darkly. "Now, doll."

I roll over obediently, showing the fact that my ass is completely bare, just some very uncomfortable bit of fabric between my legs, currently rubbing my clit every time I squirm. I whimper softly and shift my legs.

"Are you uncomfortable?" Brad asks.

I nod. "So uncomfortable. It's rubbing and..."

"And you're already soaking through, aren't you?" Carter chuckles. "Now, how do we unwrap our gift?"

"You should start. Our little slut got this for you," Brad says, waving his hand over me. "Especially since I'm tempted to *rip* it off."

Carter pushes Brad away; excitement glints in his eyes as he moves beside me. His fingers hook under a strap, pulling slightly, and a moan spills from my lips. His hold slackens, and his fingers brush to my hip, tugging on another piece, right on the one that rubs over my clit. My legs shake as I try to move, but his other hand comes down fast, cutting through the air as he slaps my thigh.

I gasp at the burn, my back arching off the ground as his fingers move with the fabric toward my clit.

"This is where you want me?" Teasingly he pulls the strap from my skin, from my pussy, and I silently nod.

He grins as he releases it, and the tight red fabric slaps on my pussy, making me cry and turn from his touch.

Carter grabs my legs, shoving them open, and with a simple nod, Brad comes closer, holding me down by my shoulders.

The bulge in Brad's pants edges closer as Carter continues his torture with the straps.

But they aren't the only ones that can play this game. I turn slightly, grazing my lips over Brad's pants, feeling the hardness beneath, and run my tongue over it.

"Fuck," Brad moans, the sound raking through my body and my nipples tighten almost painfully.

My hips buck as the rad fabric tortures my clit further, rubbing over it by Carter's plays.

"If we don't hurry up, our little slut is going to come just from the fabric rubbing against her," Brad hisses as I nibble on his pants, wanting him to feel as needy as I feel now.

Rolling my hips against the fabric desperately, so close to what I need. I'm almost coming when they finally manage to rip the lingerie off me. Tearing it to pieces.

"Fuck me," I breathe as Carter closes in, his nose moving over my thigh to my pussy.

"All worked up already?" Carter teases and flicks his tongue over my sensitive clit. My hips buck, my walls spasm as I squirm on the ground.

"We better not waste such a sweet gift," Carter mumbles against my skin, his arms wrapping around my thighs as he has his Christmas feast.

"Plea—" My words fail as his tongue quickens over my clit, pushing me closer and closer to that epic fall.

My body shudders, my hips twitch and as he sucks harshly, pulling my clit between his lips. I scream unable to stop my orgasm from tearing free.

My breath hitches as my sight blurs, but I still hear them, I still hear Carter quickly undressing and tossing his clothes aside, and then I feel him as his lips trail over my heated skin, moving higher until I feel his cock against me.

He grabs my hips as his cock is nudged against my entrance, and then he jerks me down on his cock, filling me entirely in one go. I arch back, gasping, and blink away the fuzziness.

"Fuck, you're still so tight!" He moans against my chest. "And all ours."

"Imagine how loud you'll get to be in our apartment," Brad says, peeling his hands from my shoulders. "Make our neighbors hate us every night. Walk out with both of us and enjoy the stares."

I whimper at the thought and reach out for Brad with one hand while gripping the back of Carter's neck with the other. "Please!"

"Oh, I'm not enough?" Carter jokes, taking me harder, and my eyes roll back as I groan.

Brad shakes off his clothes and lies beside me as his brother slams into me. My legs wrapped around Carter's waist, tugging him closer as my free hand trails over Brad's, wanting to feel him too.

A squeal leaves me as Carter moves us to the side, and then Brad crawls against my back. He spreads my ass; cold liquid follows and then takes his time, stretching me as Carter slows. It's perfect, but I want them as desperate and insane as I am. I drag my nails over Brad's arm when he palms my breast, and it breaks him.

He nudges his cock beside Carter, and as Carter draws back, Brad thrusts into me and Carter quickly follows. I cry out as they use me as their fucking toy, use me as they want.

"All ours to have, enjoy, use," Brad snarls in my ear. "Our perfect little slut."

"Our doll to play with however we want," Carter agrees between panting breaths.

"Yes!" I wail, almost sobbing from the pleasure and intensity.

They're too much, always. Whether it's separately or together, they always overwhelm me.

"Fuck!" I yell.

"We're starting Christmas the right way by having our best present," Carter says between his gritted teeth.

"And we're going to have you as much as we want. This is just the start. A fucking ... fuck ... a preview," Brad agrees as he fills my cunt again. "God damn, you were made for us."

"Yes, use me! Have me!" I scream, unable to hold in anything at this point.

"Oh, we're not fucking you hard enough. Hear that, Brad?" Carter says before groaning and kissing me, biting my bottom lip, and tangling his tongue with mine. "You just won't settle for gentle, will you?"

"Stop ... restraining," I order, despite the fact I'm already on the edge. An edge I didn't even know could exist after all this.

"I think we can handle our little slut just like she needs," he growls in my ear. He adjusts his position, then slams into me at the same time Brad does. Their cocks moving in synch, destroying me.

I'm lost to pleasure. Feeling how close they are, hearing every dirty word they say, but I'm on cloud nine and only getting higher and higher.

I come again, without warning, without Brad's order, and take them both with me. Neither manages to pull out, and I don't care. I don't care about anything at all. I'm here, between two of the men I care for, and that's more than enough for me.

"Such a good girl," Carter hums, kissing across my temple.

"*Our* good girl," Brad corrects, gently kissing across my jaw.

Before I can answer them, the front door unlocks, and footsteps follow.

Fuck.

# CHAPTER THIRTY-NINE

I slowly blink myself back into focus as every bit of the orgasm leaves my body. I free myself from Carter and Brad, ready to run. If it's Mom, we're fucked. Well ... more fucked than I already am. The thought almost makes me laugh, but when my legs give out and Carter jerks his sweater over me, to try and cover me up, I realize just how bad this could be.

She just learned we've been 'dating'; she doesn't need to know how and where we go at it. My cheeks flush a bright red as I'm waiting for the scream. The gasp, the yelling.

But nothing comes. I peek around Carter and sigh in relief.

It's Daddy– Henry. If I can fuck him, I can call him by his first name.

I take a slow breath and realize that Carter and Brad are silent too, staring at him. There's no lust in the room. It got sucked out the second the door opened.

Henry stares at the floor, not even looking at us or the mess we've made of each other, and he shakes his head slowly. "Mom isn't coming home."

"Where is she?" I can be angry at her and still want her safe. "She has to ... where?"

He shrugs and takes a seat on the couch. "No idea. We had a small fight in the driveway, then she was gone. She won't return my calls, and the last text she sent was to tell me we're done. *Done*."

Brad and Carter stay quiet, and I don't know how to handle this. Am I even allowed to comfort him? I'm the one who just destroyed my family. Henry went after her, and what did I do? I cried in my room, then fucked my boyfriends while Mom is ... somewhere. Should I try to call? No. No. She doesn't even know about Henry and me, but she won't talk to him. The last thing she's going to do is talk to me. I made a mess of everything, and now Mom and Henry are paying the price while I'm here, freshly fucked with my 'boyfriends.'

"I ..." I say, struggling.

Henry leans back and rubs his forehead. "I expected a bad reaction, but I don't know where she is."

"I could try to—" I start.

"No," he immediately shuts me down.

Carter trails his fingers over my side and gently shakes his head as Brad gets up and pats Henry's shoulder, trying to cover his half-hard cock with his Christmas sweater.

What the hell are we doing? "I shouldn't have said anything. I'm sorry."

"It wasn't you, angel. This has been coming for a long time. If anything, it's overdue," he says in a soft voice.

Is there some kind of survival guide to help me deal with this? Some way for us to navigate this shitstorm that makes everything okay?

I glance at Carter, and he lets me go, but he doesn't have any answers for me or his dad.

Rubbing over my thighs, I watch as Henry closes his eyes with a deep sigh. "Not that it makes this mess any better."

"I'm sorry," I repeat.

"Katie, really, don't blame yourself for this. This is just what needed to be done. It's *obvious* things haven't been good between us. Think about it." Henry snorts, still not looking at me.

I hesitate for a few seconds, then climb onto his lap, not caring how dirty I am as the cum slicks down my legs. I want to make him feel better. I don't need to fuck him to do that, but sometimes a hug does it all. So, I hug him. Hug him with everything I have, hoping that the stiffness in his body will fade, but it doesn't.

He lifts me from his lap and sets me on the arm of the couch, still not saying a word, but he does look at me, just for a second.

Brad pats Henry's shoulder again and shrugs at me. None of us have had something like this happen. I bet there's less than a handful of people in the world who have been in this position.

After a deep breath, Henry gets up and walks away.

"I don't know what to do," I hiss at the guys.

"It's a break-up. Not much can be done," Carter assures. "But it's *not* your fault, Katie. Really. They weren't doing well. Trust me on that."

Brad nods, then starts rubbing my shoulder with one hand. "It's true. If they *were* doing well, he wouldn't have wanted you."

That doesn't help even remotely. Maybe they could have worked things out if I hadn't accepted him, if I hadn't started with *them*. And now I've lost my mom.

"I don't know what to deal with first. The fact that my mom ran or that Henry's upset. Is there any way to fix both?" I ask, looking between the guys, hoping they have the answers.

"They're adults, doll," Carter says gently. "They've been adults a long time. They'll figure out how to make things okay for themselves."

"But what if *I* can make it better."

"No," Brad says decisively. "You're not doing a thing. You said what you had to say. That's more than enough. Leave the rest to them."

I want to fix things. Not only did my mom and Henry's relationship implode, but now I can't do anything right to help Henry. He's still mad, maybe even more angry since he walked away silently.

Whimpering, I try to sort out what I'm feeling, but before I come to a conclusion, Henry returns with the bags I saw him with at the mall. He stands there, dangling it on two fingers as he watches me.

"This isn't your fault, and I'm not upset with you," Henry says clearly.

"You're not?" Tears burn my eyes as my heart stammers in my chest.

"No," he says emphatically. "This mess...I would really like to forget, for just a bit." I nod. "Okay."

He smiles reassuringly. "I bought some presents for you. I want to indulge your desires, too. The timing might not be the best, but it's Christmas, and I'm not letting a hiccup get in the way of that."

"What?" I ask, taking the bag, but not looking inside.

"Open one of your presents and see if I was ever mad at you," he insists.

I reach in, and my brow furrows as I grip something, then pull out a whip. An *actual* leather whip. I swallow slightly and hold it out as my eyes widen.

Henry nods, urging me to grab the next thing, and I reach in again, pulling out cuffs, then nipple clamps, then a gag that forces my mouth open. I squeeze my thighs together, squirming as fresh wetness pools between my legs. "This is ..."

"You asked me to punish you. That's what I'm doing," Henry says.

"Henry, I—"

He lifts my chin, stopping my words. "Daddy, angel. It will always be Daddy."

My throat constricts, and I jump up and hug him. Only this time, the tension in his body fades, and his arms wrap around me.

"I'm sorry you thought I was mad, but I truly wasn't, and I plan on proving it thoroughly."

"Now?" I ask, my voice higher than normal.

"You get what you ask for on Christmas. Get up, take off that sweater, and bend over the couch," he says, his voice dropping a few octaves. I peel the sweater from my body as

I do as he says. Bending myself over the couch, my stomach coils in excitement. I don't know where my limits lie. What I can handle, but I hope I can find out. *With them.*

With the armrest blocking my view, I hear the rummaging of the bag and the soft mumbles as the guys go over a plan.

"Since we both know I like your hands still... Carter, grab her arms," Daddy orders, and goosebumps rise on my skin.

Carter obeys, taking my hands as my heart races in my chest.

"Brad, do I really have to say it?" Daddy demands, and a dark chuckle follows.

Cold metal wraps around my wrists and the sound of them tightening makes me shiver. Once there's no chance of me slipping free, my wrists are dropped uselessly to the couch.

"So pretty, all stretched out and ready to be punished," Daddy croons. "My own little whore."

I flinch as he palms my ass. "For teasing us like you do, touching us while your mother was a few feet away. For even thinking I didn't want you," he snaps and his hand leaves. The sound of leather cutting through the air follows, and then the whip comes down on my ass. I wail as my body spasms. The bite of the leather burns more than I thought it would.

I pant, each ragged breath rubbing my nipples against the couch. "Such a pretty sound," he groans, and it comes again. The leather slaps over my heated skin.

I whimper, biting my bottom lip as my arousal drips down my thighs. "Spread your legs. I'm going to watch how wet you get, until you're dripping for me," Daddy groans.

I spread my legs obediently until I feel like I'm dangling on the edge of the couch.

"Look how pretty, how slick."

Another lash, and another, and a third until I can't keep it in. I scream, and cry as my thighs tremble and my wetness drips down. The pain should turn me off, but fuck, it doesn't.

The tip of the whip trails over my spine, all the way back down to my round ass. I moan softly as the leather caresses me, so much lighter than any lashing.

Back and forth, he switches from light strokes and harsh bites until I'm begging. "Please, I'll be good! I'll be so good. I'll do whatever you want!"

I hear a thunk and wonder if the whipping is done. I squeal as I'm flipped over without a word. My gaze snaps to Daddy, he's got rid of his shirt, his pants open as his hard cock tries to break free. He dangles the nipple clamps with the chain in front of me and I swallow.

"We're just getting started, angel. And if you're a good slut, you won't have the whip anymore. If you're not.... well, I love turning that gorgeous ass into a work of art."

I wet my lips and quickly nod. I watch as he spreads one nipple clamp and edges closer, but as I move slightly, Brad and Carter grab my shoulders, keeping me still.

Daddy tugs on my nipple, making a hard peak and then attaches the clamp, gently.

"Fuck," I hiss as he releases the clamp, and it tightens. An electric spark shoots to my clit, and a breathy moan falls out of me. The pain and pleasure become the same. When he does the same to the other, I groan, and my pussy tightens with need.

Glancing to the side, Carter and Brad watching intensely, their cocks hiding for me. Why did they put on their boxers again?

Daddy grabs the chain that connects my nipples and tugs. Another electric spark shoots to my clit, and my eyes roll back, my toes curl, and I squirm on the couch.

Daddy chuckles. "So desperate to be used and fucked. I think the three of us can take care of that."

Brad smirks. "We're very good at taking care of all our little slut's needs."

"Doll, are you going to be a good girl for us?" Carter asks.

"Of course she is," Daddy answers before I can. "She didn't get to finish with me this morning. She remembers how it felt."

Them talking about me like I don't have a say makes it even hotter. I'm just here to be used, to be pleased and please them too.

I can't wait.

# CHAPTER FORTY

Daddy runs one finger over my clit and down to my dripping pussy. He slides a second with the first and opens me up, spreading me for his eyes specifically. "Your pussy definitely needs to be fucked again, doesn't it?"

"Yes!" I cry.

"And your cute little ass," his fingers trail down, and he pushes one of his thick fingers into my ass. I mewl in response, and he groans. "You're already so ready for it. You love being a dirty girl for us, don't you, angel?"

"Yes!"

"Yes, what?" he demands.

"Yes, Daddy. I want to be a good slut," I answer without hesitation.

I don't dare to move as he keeps working his single finger into my ass. But I want more. I *need* more.

I whimper and look back at my stepbrothers. "Please?"

"You don't get to decide and those two aren't going to move until I let them," Daddy says. "If you're going to beg, beg, but I'm the only one who can give you what you want right now."

My thighs tremble, nearly closing around his hand.

"Keep these legs open while I look at you, while I watch what one single finger in your ass does to you," he purrs.

My face heats as I turn my gaze to his. "Please, Daddy? I want to be fucked so badly. I'll be good. I promise."

"I know you will, because you like to please Daddy, don't you?" he asks, working a second finger into my ass.

I can barely get words out when he's touching me and putting on a show for the same two men who just had me by the Christmas tree. "Yes, Daddy."

"Spread your legs wider," he orders while tugging on the chain between my breasts again.

I moan and obey, spreading my legs as wide as I possibly can in this position while I feel the couch brushing over my sore ass cheeks.

Daddy groans. "That's a good girl. I'm thinking your *boyfriends* get to watch while I fuck your sweet pussy, angel. Then, as long as you and *your boyfriends* behave, you'll have all of us."

"Yes, please, please, Daddy," I beg again.

He holds onto the chain that tugs on my nipples and frees his cock. Pre-cum leaks from the tip, and I tilt my hips as he inches closer. I bite my bottom lip as he rubs himself over my pussy, teasing me with what I could have.

He chuckles. "You're already shaking. I bet you'd come from this alone if you're desperate enough."

"Please," I cry, and move my hips again.

He grips his cock and taps my entrance twice, taunting me further as his fingers curl lower, thrusting in my ass again.

My back curves, my eyes close and then he rams into me.

"Oh fu—" I start to scream as his thick cock fills me to the brim. I can't breathe, can't speak, can't do anything as my pussy stretches around him.

"So fucking wet," he groans.

He draws back and thrusts into me again, nearly bending me in half. My breasts bounce making the chain tighten again, and I almost come. I'm still held into place as we three watch how Daddy plows into me over and over.

Moans tear from my throat until I'm afraid I'm going to go hoarse. My ass clamps around his fingers every time he thrusts into me.

"You don't get to come without my permission, angel. You have to beg. If you try, it's back to the whip," he warns and slaps my sore ass with his other hand.

I whimper and nod weakly. "Yes, I'll beg, Daddy. Oh!"

He hits that sweet spot deep inside me and my hips lift off the couch. I can't take it. I can't hold back. His fingers, his cock, every dirty word. "Please let me come, Daddy."

"No," he jerks away, leaving me entirely empty.

My lips part. Carter and Brad's hands peel away from me. "But—"

"Roll onto the floor," he orders sharply. "Do you want your boyfriends to play with you too? Aren't you their 'doll'? Their 'little slut'?" he asks darkly.

"Yes, Daddy," I answer and scamper to the floor, whimpering as the chain tugs on the clamps again.

Getting on my hands and knees, arching my back as I glance over my shoulder at Daddy. He groans and traces his fingers over the marks on my skin. "We'll have to be gentle with you later, take care of your pretty ass so you can sit and open presents."

Before I can speak, Daddy looks at Carter. "You want to get under her, or should we hold her up?"

"Under." Carter flings his boxer off and lays down, and I crawl over him.

"Take his cock and put him inside you," Daddy orders.

I obey, without question. Carter hisses when I rub my fingers over his hard dick, then I slide down him, feeling him settle in. He grips my hips and bites the chain between my breasts, tugging it, and my walls clench around his cock.

"Gripping me so tight, doll," he teases and thrusts slowly.

Daddy kneels behind me, nudging his cock against my ass and works himself inside me. He doesn't give me time, nudging further and then he's fully inside me, spreading my ass around him.

I cry out, as my body breaks between them.

"How is your ass this tight, angel? I'm sure at least one of my boys has been in here," Daddy laughs. "Fuck us. Show us how badly you want us."

I obey, thrusting against them, grinding my hips, circling them, trying to take them how I want to, but neither are moving. It's torture in the best way.

"Please!" I beg.

"Oh, I thought you wanted to be in control, telling me what you needed, what you wanted. You don't like it?" Daddy asks mockingly.

"I want you in charge," I say shakily.

"It's what you need, angel," he agrees before drawing almost all the way out of my ass and slamming back into me.

I gasp. Carter bites the chain so hard I hear it, then jerks it again. Every tug on my nipples, the way they fuck me, it's too much. I tremble as I try to hold myself together, knowing Daddy won't let me come, until all three of them are inside me some way or another.

"Such a naughty girl, leaving Brad to take care of himself. Do you see him stroking his cock? I bet he's wondering if he can fill your pussy with his brother," Daddy says in my ear darkly. "I don't think you can manage it. You're just too tight."

"I ..."

"He's going to take your throat. You're going to gag on him, and you won't be able to come until after you make him come," Daddy snarls.

That's all it takes to have Brad filling my throat. I look up at him as my eyes water. It's emotional, physical, everything overload. He grits his teeth and slams into my throat again, choking me on his cock until I gag. He draws back, and with a wicked smile he thrust inside my mouth again.

"Looks like you're going to have to wait a long time at that pace, angel. You'll have to work a lot harder if you want to come."

I try to move forward, to take some kind of control with Brad. I need his cum so I can come too. My thighs are shaking and my pussy spasms around Carter. Pulling his cock deeper and deeper.

My eyes don't stay open. I moan and move around Brad's dick faster, sucking him harder, licking and deepthroating, giving him everything I can offer.

"Look how eager she is. You're right to call her a slut. She has three men and still wants more," Daddy says before swatting my bottom, and I moan, the sound vibrating around Brad's cock.

"All sweaty and red already?" Brad teases, gripping my hair tightly. "You haven't finished any of us. Work harder. Show me how good that mouth is."

I pant, trying to keep my eyes open as I take them all. Daddy's so rough with me, plowing into me unrelentingly, and Carter's no different. Brad's the one holding back, torturing me, because he knows he can. I want to change that. I want all of them filling me up with their cum. I want to please all three. *Make them proud.*

My jaw hurts, my throat is raw, and tears roll down my face. Gagging on Brad's attack and then he comes, pushing deep down my throat, choking me as he holds me in place until every last drop of his cum is sliding down my throat.

I wheeze for air as he pulls out and beg once more. "Please let me come!"

"You've almost come twice," Daddy accuses, spanking my sore and bruised ass again. "Did you think the boys groaning would hide it? I felt your ass get tight."

"I didn't come! I want to, please. Please. I'm so close! Please, Daddy! Please, let me come!" I wail.

He groans and ups the pace. Every thrust is impossibly fast and deep, threatening to make me come even though I don't have permission.

It *hurts* to hold out.

Finally, he growls between his teeth. "Come! Come right now, angel or you'll wait until tomorrow."

I let go of my restraint and come, my pussy gripping Carter like a vice and my ass tightening around Daddy until they're all I feel. I scream as I come. I gush over their cocks, nearly pass out right there.

Carter moves his mouth and bites my breast as he lets out a long groan and grinds into me rather than actually fucking me. I feel the warm spray of his cum fill me. Daddy's next. After ramming into me again and again, he stops, pulls his cock almost all the way out, then finishes inside my ass. It breaks me, and I collapse on top of Carter, panting, squirming, unable to stop my body from spasming and twitching.

Brad lifts my chin and winks. "Such a good slut."

"Daddy's good girl," Daddy agrees while lightly patting my back.

# Chapter Forty-One

## *A few days later*

I never heard back from my mom, well, nothing other than the one text message.

*MOM: Katie, stop calling me! I can't believe you did this to me. How could you have turned into this person? Sleeping with both your brothers. One, I could accept. But two. I can't be around you. What will people think?! Don't you care about me at all!*

I do care, but I can't control who I fall in love with.

Even if that love was kind of forced on me. And still, if I could go back, I wouldn't want to change it. I have two men who love me. And then there is Henry.

I might not know what the future brings, but I'm dying to find out.

There's one thing I do know, and that is Henry isn't coming with us. And I understand that.

His life is here. He still wants some closure with my mom. He knows there is nothing there anymore, and he doesn't want to fix it. But he can't stop his entire life to live with me.

There's this side of me that's disappointed that he doesn't come, but I do know that my feelings for Brad and Carter are stronger. And that they are the ones I want to spend my life with. Or at least try. You never know. Maybe in a few months, they'll get sick of me and leave.

I really hope they don't, or that this isn't all some elaborate play from Brad.

A soft laugh leaves me as I shake my head, packing my last clothes. Maybe I'm wrong in all this, and maybe I care more about Henry than I want to admit. Because there is one thing I learned about myself. *I sometimes don't realize what I truly want.*

"What am I missing?" Brad asks and wraps his arms around my waist, pulling my back against him.

"I was just thinking about your games."

His body tenses, and he turns me in his grip. "This isn't a game."

I smile. "I know."

His brows twitch as I see that glint of doubt again. "I'm not playing a game," I add.

He softly sighs, and the uncertainty fades. He's so strong, and so wicked in his plays but can be insecure when it comes to me. As if he fears I don't care the same way he does.

I bite the inside of my cheek as I free myself from his hold. "Can you get Carter?"

He nods. "Sure." He doesn't linger as he steps out of my room, calling Carter to get his ass up here.

There is one thing I have to do before we leave and follow the path we set up for ourselves. Some simple words I hadn't said yet.

All because I was scared.

Scared of them, but more scared of myself. Of this person who was hiding inside me for all these years. This woman with her crazy desires.

The woman they showed me.

I shouldn't make a big deal out of this. Perhaps I even said it once before. I'm not really sure, but I do know that the meaning of it has changed because now I truly love them. I couldn't love them before, not when I didn't even know who I truly was.

Brad comes back inside with Carter close behind him, and a nervous smile tugs on my lips.

"I need you both to hear this, really hear this," I say, gesturing to my bed for them to take a seat.

With confusion in their eyes, they gaze at each other before taking their seats.

I fidget with my hands as they stare at me, waiting for what I might say.

"I realized I might have," I start, but nothing else comes. My face heats, my palms turn sweaty, but my next words won't come as Brad cuts me off.

"You're not coming. You don't want to live with us. That's it, right?"

I quickly shake my head. "No, that isn't what I wanted to say."

"You only want Brad?" Carter asks.

"No—" I start again.

"I know I've been busy this Christmas break, and we didn't spend enough time together, but I promise that was because I was finalizing the last details for our new place." He rakes his fingers through his hair.

I step closer, my hands midair. "I know, Carter. And I'm really—"

"You want to stay with Dad?" Brad spits out.

"Oh god, this is it..."

They keep spitting their words as I keep stammering until Brad gets up and storms past me.

"No! Shut up you two! I'm here trying to tell you I love you!"

Silence. Deafening silence. The kind that crawls up your skin and tightens around your throat.

"Sit your ass down!" I spit at Brad, and he walks back, carefully sitting beside Carter again.

"I don't want out. I want this to work because I don't see a future without you two. I love you two." I breathe.

"You love me?" Brad asks first.

"Yes, I do, and I also love Carter." The steadiness in my voice is back and my heart follows.

Carter is quick and closes the distance between us in a blink. His arms haul me against him as he hugs me tightly. "Finally, doll. I feared you would never say it."

"Sorry it took me so long." I chuckle and reach for Brad, who still sits frozen on my bed.

"You love me?" he asks again as he takes my hand.

"Weird right?" Carter jokes. "My little brother, loved."

I slap Carter's chest and tug Brad closer. "Don't tease him like that!"

This is how it's going to be, right? Us having fun. Being our own family.

The warmth of their bodies seeps into mine, and all the nerves I had disappear into nothing. A soft creak at the door makes me inch back. Henry leans against the doorframe, a tense smile on his lips.

"Are you ready to go?" he asks, and Carter and Brad release their hold on me, but stay close.

"We are," I say. "Are you okay?"

His hair is a mess, his beard desperately needs some attention, and the bags under his eyes make my ribs tighten.

"Always." His smile widens, but I don't buy it. There's something in his eyes. This sadness that breaks through me.

"I'm sure going to miss you, angel," he says as he crosses his arms over his chest.

I take a shaky breath, taking my chance, knowing this might hurt me.

"You don't have to," I say.

He scoffs. "We already talked about this. I can't come."

"No, you talked, and I listened, but you never asked me what I wanted."

He blinks, pushes himself off the doorway, and crawls closer. "Then what do you want?"

I swallow as he towers over me, his eyes searching mine for the answer. And I hesitantly reach for his cheek, grazing my fingers over his skin. "I want you." I pause, peeling my fingers away and taking Carter and Brad's hand.

"I might be selfish, but I don't care." Tightening my grip on their hands, I peek up at Henry's eyes.

"I want all of you."

He stares down at me, a storm raging through his eyes until they fill.

A single tear rolls down his cheek, and he slumps to his knees, wrapping his arms around my hips.

"I'm all yours, angel," he whispers and gently kisses my mound.

Surrounded by the men who love me and crave me with their darkest desires, all of me, is more than I could ever wished for.

"Let's go home," I say. "Our new home."

**—THE END—**

Printed in Great Britain
by Amazon